
★ ·

"SEX, MONEY OR REVE
SAL

"I think it's time to ch_____
ing to take a run do_____
there's no reason I sh_____
for an actor to kill Hu_____

"I still don't see why all the dressing up."

"It's the first thing that would occur to an actor.
How do you get away with murder? Dress up as
someone else. Let's try a little identification parade. I want you to take that kid from the motel to
see the play, see if any of the actors look familiar.
Tell him to imagine them all with a gold tooth and
sunglasses."

"You mean I have to see that play again?"

"You missed most of it last time. It'll be an experience."

"The whole play?"

"Unless he makes an ID in the first five minutes."

—————————— ★ ——————————

*"For those who like their mysteries on the
subdued side . . . Charlie Salter is an ideal
companion."*

—Booklist

Also available from Worldwide Mystery by
ERIC WRIGHT

FINAL CUT
A SENSITIVE CASE
A QUESTION OF MURDER

Forthcoming from Worldwide Mystery by
ERIC WRIGHT

DEATH BY DEGREES

ERIC WRIGHT
A FINE ITALIAN HAND

WORLDWIDE®

TORONTO • NEW YORK • LONDON
AMSTERDAM • PARIS • SYDNEY • HAMBURG
STOCKHOLM • ATHENS • TOKYO • MILAN
MADRID • WARSAW • BUDAPEST • AUCKLAND

If you purchased this book without a cover you should be aware
that this book is stolen property. It was reported as "unsold and
destroyed" to the publisher, and neither the author nor the
publisher has received any payment for this "stripped book."

A FINE ITALIAN HAND

A Worldwide Mystery/May 1994

This edition is reprinted by arrangement with Charles
Scribner's Sons, an imprint of Macmillan Publishing
Company.

ISBN 0-373-26143-8

Copyright © 1992 by Eric Wright.
All rights reserved. No part of this book may be reproduced
or transmitted in any form or by any means, electronic or
mechanical, including photocopying, recording or by any
information storage and retrieval system, without permission
in writing from the publisher. For information, contact:
Charles Scribner's Sons, 866 Third Avenue, New York,
NY 10022 U.S.A.

All characters in this book are fictitious, and any resemblance to
actual persons, living or dead, is purely coincidental.

® and TM are trademarks of Harlequin Enterprises Limited.
Trademarks indicated with ® are registered in the United States
Patent and Trademark Office, the Canadian Trade Marks Office
and in other countries.

Printed in U.S.A.

For Tony and Janet Harold

PROLOGUE

THE BLUE VOLKSWAGEN JETTA was parked against the wall behind the motel. It was a tourist's car, or even a salesman's, not the kind of car the regular customers would be seen alive in.

The clerk checked the license plates and flipped through his registration cards. Most of the night's arrivals had scrawled something indecipherable, leaving the license space blank. It was that kind of motel. The occasional tourist or salesman who wandered into this part of the jungle usually filled out the card properly, but there was no record of the Jetta.

The car was hidden from the view of anyone in the motel and the clerk had only noticed it when he took out the night's garbage. He checked through the windows and saw that it was empty except for a woman's scarf on the rear window ledge, and a striped umbrella with a wooden handle on the back seat. The sun visor on the driver's side was pulled down as if the owner had been using the mirror. The car doors and the trunk were locked.

After he had checked the registrations, the clerk propped open the door of the office so that he could watch for the appearance of the owner, but by nine-thirty he knew he had to check the bedrooms. He found the body in number five, a once good-looking man in his late thirties with a length of sash cord still around his neck and blood from his wounds soaking into the bedcovers. The clerk locked the door and telephoned the police.

ONE

'YOU EVER GO TO PLAYS, Salter? On stage?'

Staff Inspector Charlie Salter wondered where the question was coming from. He was in the office of his immediate superior, a deputy chief of the Metropolitan Toronto Police. He was expecting to be reprimanded, promoted, retired, or transferred to the marine unit. He was unaware of what he had done to deserve any of this.

The summons had come without explanation. Now it was beginning to sound as if he had been suggested as a likely person to put on a skit at the annual police ball. I'll retire, he thought. On the spot.

'Not much,' he said.

On the other hand, maybe the deputy had been given a couple of free tickets to the current show at the Royal Alex, and didn't know what to do with them?

'How come?' the deputy demanded.

Salter stared back at him, having already forgotten the question. That morning he had been wakened at five when the one-bird spring chorus started up outside his bedroom window. He had slept well until then, and the paper had already been delivered, so he went downstairs and made himself a cup of coffee and returned to bed to see if he liked starting the day like that. It wasn't bad, he decided, but he actually preferred juice before his coffee, and if he went that far he might as well take the toast to bed, too, which would mean putting the marmalade on first, and being very careful not to get marmalade on the paper and then on to the sheets, because if Annie, his wife, returned to a bed full of breadcrumbs and marmalade she would wonder what the hell had been going on. Annie was a thousand miles away, on Prince Edward Island, where she was visiting her father who had been felled by a stroke.

By the time the sun was level with the bedroom window Salter was thinking about fishing—the pickerel season opened soon—and the way in which spring, in Canada, can overnight bring back the sounds and the scents and the pulse to a land that has died of exposure, and he tried to remember some of the words of one of the few poems that had ever affected him, Roethke's 'A Field of Light', because he had seen for once how poetry worked, and the rebirth evoked in the poem happened in exactly that way every year on a morning like this, and once again he wondered why all the great spring myths came from Greece or thereabouts, where pre-spring wasn't nearly so bad as in Canada, which ought by rights to have a monopoly on myths about the dramatic return of life when the sap rises in the maples; and Salter wished Annie were here, in bed beside him, and then it was eight o'clock and he was late.

'How come you haven't been to many plays?' the deputy repeated.

Because they weren't there, Salter thought. He shrugged, feeling no requirement to defend himself. 'It looks as if I'll have to start going. My kid wants to be an actor. Thinks he is one already.'

'You don't know this guy, then?' The deputy held up a picture cut from a newspaper.

'Alec Hunter,' Salter said.

The deputy nodded. 'He's dead. You know that?'

'I heard.'

Everybody had. Hunter had been found stabbed and garrotted in a motel on the lakeshore. At the time, he had just finished playing the lead in a new Canadian play, a part in which he had had a considerable success, only relinquishing it because he had a previous commitment in a movie.

'Somebody told me you knew him. He was in that movie you were advising on last year when the scriptwriter got stabbed.'

Salter reached for the picture and held it at the right distance from his eyes. 'Yeah. He was an extra, one of the heavies. He was only in one scene. He was supposed to be beating up the hero.'

The deputy picked up a clipping. 'He's called "well-known" in this story. Not just an extra.'

'He was a bit player. He had two lines, I think.'

'Two lines? So why do they call him well-known?'

'I think they mean well-known locally. On the stage. Here. In Toronto. Not on TV.'

'Says here he played the lead.'

'Yeah?' Salter tried to think of an extra response. He had said everything he had to say about Alec Hunter, but the deputy had the habit of not taking 'don't know' for an answer, continuing to rephrase the question on the apparent assumption that if he got the words of the question right then the answer would come. 'You know the press,' Salter tried.

'But if he played the lead then he couldn't be a bit player, could he?'

Salter said nothing, contenting himself with a bemused look and a little headshake.

The deputy continued to stare at him, waiting for him to break down and confess. 'Maybe plays and movies use different terms,' he said.

Salter nodded eagerly. 'That's what I figure.'

'Why is that?'

It's just a style, Salter thought. If your rank entitles you to a captive audience, then you can think out loud. It only sounds like interrogation. The thing to do is to let him go on, stare back, smile, say nothing.

'They should've said well-known *stage* actor, right?' the deputy said.

Salter didn't flinch.

'I mean, for most people, "actor" means movies, right?'

Salter said nothing.

'You say he just had little bitty parts in movies?'

'In the movie I was involved with.'

'Maybe he was well-known from other movies?'

Don't even blink, Salter told himself.

'I reckon that's about the size of it.' The deputy leaned back, waiting.

If I even nod, Salter thought, he'll ask me how come he played a bit part if he's so well known. The last time Salter felt this way he was four years old and being teased by a creepy uncle who thought putting a series of unanswerable conundrums to a child was funny. But there was no hint of a twinkle about Deputy Chief Mackenzie. He was just sorting out his head.

Now the deputy nodded, satisfied he had got to the bottom of it. 'Anyway, he's dead. Knifed and strangled.'

'Drugs?'

Mackenzie shook his head. 'I don't think so. He didn't use them. And no one is saying he dealt them.'

'Gambling?'

'Why d'ya say that?'

Because I'm bored, Salter thought. Because even from here I think I can smell the lilac at the other end of the parking lot. Why didn't he get on with it? What did he want from Salter? 'It's one of the ways outsiders get tangled up with the mob. Losing big bets. The other way is through drugs.'

'Why do you say "mob"?'

'I heard the guy was strangled, garrotted with a cord or a wire. Isn't that their trademark?'

'Whose?'

Salter blinked. 'The Mafia. Cosa Nostra. Our Thing.'

'Not some Greek gang? Or Jamaican? Or Portuguese?'

'Do they strangle people?'

'Who?'

'The Greeks, Jamaicans, Portuguese.'

'Why not?'

'Christ knows, sir, but when you hear garrotted you don't think Greek, or Jamaican, or Portuguese. You think Italian.'

'Ah... ah... ah.' The deputy let out his breath and nodded four or five times. 'That's my problem. Everybody thinks mob, thinks Italian, even you. Now forget you said that. Start with a clean notebook. OK?'

'To do what?'

'Didn't I say? I'm putting you in charge.'

'Don't we have a Homicide unit any more?'

'Yes, we do and you're going to join it, temporarily.'

'What about the "position paper"?' Salter asked in reference to a study he was working on.

'Give this priority.'

'Why?'

'Because Marinelli suggested you.' Staff Sergeant Marinelli was acting as head of the Homicide unit while the unit inspector was on vacation. 'You know why, don't you?'

Salter shook his head. 'I've been on leave.'

'I thought you'd caught up with the scuttlebutt. You knew the guy was strangled.'

'That was in the papers.'

'All right. Here it is. This guy, Alec Hunter, was found dead three days ago in a motel. One of our leading crime reporters—I'll give you three guesses who—got to the motel clerk who reported the incident. One of the things the clerk told him was that the team from Homicide said it looked like a mob killing. What our guy actually said, according to the clerk as reported by the ace reporter, was that it looked like the handiwork of the Italians. So the reporter goes for a story with a heading, "A Fine Italian Hand, police say".'

'Why did he put it like that?'

'It's a quotation, they tell me. This reporter reads a
lot. So my phone starts ringing. Just about every Italian of any consequence in the city is after our ass, all
the way up to, but not yet including, the consul. Point
is they are sick and tired of being smeared any time
anything illegal happens. So Staff Sergeant Marinelli—get the name—issues a statement denying the
guy said anything like that, and insisting they have no
evidence to link the killing with any particular ethnic
group, and that if our guy mentioned Italian, he also
mentioned Portuguese, Vietnamese and several other
possibilities. But the clerk is sure of what he heard,
and anyway the clerk himself offered the information
that the room had been rented by a guy with an Italian accent. This was something we didn't know yet—
the Italian accent, I mean—so the reporter runs another story about Marinelli denying any Italian connection and having no comment to make about the
guy with the Italian accent which he'd only just heard
about from the reporter. So now we have half the
population—the Italians—calling us racist, and the
other half thinking we're in bed with the mob. The way
the reporter wrote the story he mentioned Marinelli's
name half-a-dozen times. Now Marinelli's ready to go
out and garrotte the reporter, but I told him that won't
help. If he has to, I told him, use an ice-axe and we'll
blame it on a Scandinavian mob. Marinelli, by the
way, does not even speak Italian. His family came over
from Milan before the First World War.'

'Who was the officer who mentioned Italian in the
first place?'

'He's a new guy, new to Homicide, anyway.'

'What's his name?'

'Bardetski. He's been shifted so this reporter can't get to him.'

'So put together a new team. Use a black detective and that Greek woman sergeant in 55 Division.'

'I'm putting you on it. I've already told all these Italian aldermen that I have appointed a senior investigator to coordinate the inquiry in view of the possibility that various factions might be involved—gambling, drugs, and so on.'

'Do we know what he was doing in the motel?'

'The guy's wife or whatever said he was a gambler and he was probably meeting someone he had to pay off. She had given him a thousand the day before. As far as she knew, that night he was supposed to be visiting his great-aunt in an old folks' home. That was the last she saw of him. There was no money on him when he was found.'

'Who found him?'

'Yeah, I know. The same desk clerk at the motel. He had lots of time to look around and hide a thousand dollars while he was waiting for us.'

'And who was "us" in the first instance?'

'Forget that. A two-man squad, or rather, Constable Dunham and a woman, Constable Perry, both squeaky clean. She's factory fresh, just out of training. It doesn't matter a helluva lot, though, does it? We're after a homicide. Point I want to make is that—who do you know on the gambling detail?'

'Lindstrom; Joe Horvarth. Why?'

Mackenzie nodded. 'They'll tell you what you want to know. Joe has a lot of contacts.'

'Homicide must have completed all the preliminary work,' Salter said. 'Who else was on the case?'

'Sergeant Peterman. We're leaving him on it. But go to Marinelli. He'll fill you in.'

SALTER LEFT the deputy's office and went in search of the lilacs. Already he had almost forgotten what the deputy had called him in for; all his receptors were focused inwards. Waking so early that morning, he had tried to know if his desire for Annie was a sign of life or a reaction to his recurring fear of old age, loneliness and death. Her absence had given him a lot of time, not to think, exactly, but to look at and be aware of such thoughts as they occurred, put him in a musing mood, separating him from the world around him. Simply being alone did that, but the reason for her absence added. Her father had had a stroke, might be dying. Her mother had turned useless and dependent. Annie's two brothers' wives responded dutifully, but kept their distance. It was a daughter's place to look after her mother; so seemed to say her mother, and the daughters-in-law silently agreed. So Annie had flown back to Charlottetown three weeks ago, and looked liked staying forever, needing time to educate her mother out of the notion that her need for Annie was greater than that of Salter's family. Annie's mother was a former English teacher with whom Salter had no emotional ties. He had thought he liked her once, in spite of her habit of trotting out quotations as a critical commentary on the passing scene ('Provoke not your children to anger,' she intoned once, when Salter was quarreling with his sons, 'lest they be discouraged.') but over the years he had become aware that she regarded his work as embarrassing, not appropriate for a member of her clan; real men worked in business like her husband and her sons, and besides, if Salter would only accept the standing and frequently-referred-to offer of a job with the family business, then Annie would be back on the Island, near her mother, where she belonged.

From the beginning Salter had resisted being absorbed by the Montagus, by their assumption that the Salters would spend all their holidays on the Island, for example. But now, in crisis, the pressure from the whimsical iron-willed matriarch was so powerful that Salter had decided to give up Annie if necessary, to resist it. It wouldn't come to that, though, would it? Perhaps it wasn't entirely *his* mother-in-law. Perhaps it was always like this, for everybody. As soon as the children stop making demands, the grandparents start. Was there no space in between for a tiny second honeymoon? Thinking such thoughts, Salter wanted to take Annie off to that Oxfordshire inn where they had arrived years ago in the early afternoon to a room fragrant with gilly-flowers and they had celebrated in a bed so soft that he had made love to her on his knees like a character in a Rowlandson cartoon, with the scent of the flowers pouring through the casement window.

Salter looked around for the lilacs but there had never been any lilacs in the parking lot; he was still dreaming, had not stopped since he woke up that morning. Lilacs, for God's sake. Even the lilac tree in Salter's garden had been cut down twenty years before.

TWO

STAFF SERGEANT MARINELLI was waiting for him in
his office. When Salter arrived, he called in a man
from the outer office and introduced him. 'This is
Dick Peterman. He and Bardetski were on the case
until Bardetski got chatty. Staff Inspector Salter.'

The two men knew each other by sight, but they
shook hands to signal the start of a new enterprise.
Salter was wary at this stage. It was not the first time
he had investigated a homicide: the circumstances had
always had to be unusual for him to be assigned instead of the regular investigators, and at least twice the
Homicide unit had not seen the necessity for Salter's
involvement, and he had had to begin in the face of
some hostility; but on one of those cases he had ended
up on better terms with Marinelli than he had started
with. Now he watched for signs that Peterman had
taken up an attitude. 'I understand me being here is
your idea,' he said to Marinelli, in case Peterman had
not heard.

Marinelli caught the point immediately. 'I already
explained to Dick. We really don't need any help but
the deputy is getting the pressure and the reporters
would harrass Bardetski into the ground, so I asked
for someone to take the heat. When Mackenzie asked
me if I had any suggestions, I said you'd worked with

us before. Special Affairs. That's what you're all about. Right, sir?'

Marinelli was sending a complicated message. To start with, he was saying that they didn't need Salter, that his being there was someone else's idea. Solidarity, for Peterman's benefit. Secondly, he was saying that, nevertheless, he did not question the deputy's judgement: matters of politics were not Marinelli's concern. That's what deputies were paid for. Thirdly, he was reminding Peterman that he, Marinelli, preferred Salter to some unknown alternative. And that said, he was adding a tiny note of mockery about Salter's unit, the derision of a troop commander for someone who did not normally come up to the front line.

Peterman said, 'How will we work it? Are we some kind of team? Or will you look after the reporters while I go back to work?'

His attitude was more curious than hostile. This was all new to him, and he really wanted to know what to expect.

Salter said, 'Are you on this case full-time?'

Marinelli laughed. 'Where've you been, Charlie? We've had two shootouts in Chinatown in the last ten days, a Sikh assassinated, a gay accountant murdered, and a pillar of Rosedale society put a contract out on his girlfriend. How many cases you on, Dick?'

Again Salter caught the message, which was to use Salter's first name to show Peterman that there was no real distance between them. They had not in fact been on first name terms before.

'Two,' Peterman said. 'One of the shootouts, and a drifter who was kicked to death in a rooming-house two days ago, and this makes three.' He looked at Salter with a bland expression. All the messages had been received, his face said. He would go along with anything the other two suggested.

On the whole, Salter was reassured. Unless Peterman was a very good poker player, the arrival of Salter did not bother him. He was a professional and he had done his job properly. His colleague, Bardetski, had created a temporary difficulty due to his inexperience in dealing with reporters, a difficulty it was Salter's job to take care of. Salter saw Peterman glance at his watch and took that as a further sign that the sergeant had no special tension about Salter. There were other things on his mind.

Peterman was in his late thirties, dark-haired and balding in front. His cheeks were smooth and shiny and slightly flushed. His shoulders were narrow for his weight, which was settling slightly around his waist. He had heavy thighs, shortish legs and small feet in brightly polished shoes. In five years, unless he did something about it, he would have an egg of a head on top of a pear-shaped body. He did not seem a man to be fussed.

'Let's move into my office,' Salter said. 'You can fill me in there.' He yawned. 'Sorry. I didn't get enough sleep last night.'

Peterman looked squarely at his watch. 'Can I have five minutes?' he asked, and stood up.

As he reached the door, Marinelli said, 'Keep me in touch, Dick.'

Another message. Marinelli and Peterman were colleagues; Salter was the outsider.

SALTER HAD TIME to get settled behind his desk and move the project he was working on to one side before Peterman arrived. He had been making a study of the relationship between the police and the two levels of government that most concerned them, the metropolitan and the provincial. His instructions were to analyse the relationships as they existed now and as they might be about to change. Two things precipitated the need for such a study. Ontario had just elected a socialist government, part of whose mandate was to eradicate inequalities that arose from differences of gender, sexual orientation, race, colour, and ethnicity, and there was an excellent chance that the city of Toronto would soon elect a left-wing mayor, one who could be expected to have a similar agenda.

The second event was a news report that some senior officers at Scotland Yard were seriously discussing not cooperating with a Labour government should one be elected, a suggestion that had grown out of a 'think tank'.

The new government in Ontario had begun its work enthusiastically, and already one cabinet minister was under pressure to resign for interfering with a judicial process, not for the traditional reason of helping out someone who had contributed heavily to party funds, but because the judgement offended the minister's sense of social responsibility. Not all members of the new government understood clearly that the governments are not above the law, even those with the purest of motives, and the means used must be as scrupulous as the ends were worthy.

Knowing the pressures they would be facing from their new masters, and wondering if the English had anything to teach them, Salter's bosses had decided to take the initiative. As one of the deputies had said, 'Every single group in town as well as a lot of individuals are going to present us with position papers about what they think the rôle of the police is. That's what these people do: they write position papers and present them at conferences. We should do the same. Have our own position paper.'

It was then decided that the position paper should come out of a think tank, but since they had to have something to think about, Salter was delegated to prepare a study.

He was enjoying it. He found he had no particular axe to grind; that is, he could stay detached while reading about attitudes that were light years away from his own, including the idea of not cooperating with the government. In some ways, it was like being a student again, assigned to a 'project', or an essay. In another way he was back doing the kind of work he had enjoyed ten years before, before the retirement of his old boss had left him homeless. It was annoying to be interrupted to be the window-dressing for an investigation into a probably insoluble homicide.

As the sergeant came through the door, Salter adjusted his impression of him slightly. The slight covering of fat had suggested a belly, but now Salter saw that Peterman had a huge deep chest, and no waist bulging over his belt. The bulky torso was balanced on slightly too short legs ending in little feet that seemed to glide as he advanced on the desk. Only when he sat down did he seem awkward, unable or unwilling to bend to the contours of the chair. Saying nothing, he waited for his cue. When Salter nodded, he began his exposition without the help of a notebook, smoothly, addressing Salter as if reading a teleprompter on Salter's forehead.

'Alec Hunter,' he began. 'Thirty-seven, white, male, left his house at seven-thirty on Sunday night; found dead at nine-thirty Monday morning. He'd been stabbed twice, also strangled with a ligature, a piece of sash cord. The autopsy showed he died of strangulation. The knife wounds were probably administered just before or at the same time, but they were not the cause of death. He was found in the clothes he was wearing when he left home. There was no evidence of drugs, or poisons, and only so much alcohol as was consistent with the wine he had had at dinner. There was a small cut on the bridge of his nose and several small cuts inside his mouth, behind the upper lip which indicated a punch during the struggle that took place. The time of death was between twelve and eight hours previously.'

Salter said, 'Between eight and twelve hours?'

'This is Dr Vetere, the pathologist.' Peterman smiled at what he was about to say. 'He says you should record it historically, from early to late, like from ninety BC to eighty BC. He's on his own on this but it makes complete sense, so we don't change it until he goes away.'

Salter saw an opportunity to further close the gap between them. 'I knew a doctor once who claimed you should wash your hands first, *then* piss, because you can't infect yourself with your own urine but you never know where your hands have been. I've never known anyone to do it, even though it makes some kind of sense.'

'Same medical school,' Peterman agreed. He resumed. 'He was found by the clerk who called us and stayed with the body until we got there. I interviewed the clerk on duty the night before. He had never seen the victim before. The room had been rented at around eight o'clock on Sunday to a guy with black hair, sunglasses, and an Italian accent. The clerk told me about the accent in a second interview, after he'd told the press. I asked him if he knew the difference between an Italian accent, a Portuguese accent, a Greek accent and a Spanish accent. He said he couldn't be sure, but this sounded Italian to him.'

'You mean he couldn't tell the difference, or just couldn't describe it?' Salter's professional concentration was slowly returning. The lilacs were going.

Peterman looked at him warily. Salter continued, 'If you asked me, I couldn't actually describe the difference between the accents of a guy from Barcelona or one from Rome, but if I heard them I could tell you which was Spanish and which was Italian. What I'm asking is, did the clerk say the guy *seemed* Italian, which is a fact, I mean how he seemed to the clerk, and then agree he could be wrong?'

'He said he seemed Italian. I'm not sure I'm with you, Staff.'

'Never mind. Keep going.'

Peterman twirled his feet around each other and re-balanced himself on the chair. 'This Italian-seeming guy booked the room, paid cash, of course, left a phoney car registration number—said his car had a Michigan registration, but the digits were all wrong when we checked, and that was the only person the clerk saw. Next we interviewed Hunter's girlfriend, Connie Spurling. They lived together in her house. She has her own business, she's an agent, for Hunter among others, and she says Hunter was into gambling and lately she has had to pay his debts. She gave him a thousand dollars the day before on the strict understanding that this would be the last time. She thought he meant it, says he really seemed to have made up his mind to quit. Sunday night he left home around seven-thirty to visit his great-aunt in a home in the Annexe. We checked it and Hunter had called that night. Spurling never saw or heard from him again.'

'What's she like? This Spurling woman?'

'You mean, how did she seem? To me?' Peterman smiled. 'Not bad-looking. Good paint job. Hard. Stringy. Expensive. And all racked up. Really racked up. She kept insisting that she'd done all she could, that it wasn't her fault. I had the feeling that she'd only given the money after a lot of pressure, but she *had* given it to him, so she couldn't be blamed, could she? That was her real concern. If she'd given him the money earlier, maybe, then he would still be alive. I also got the impression that she was really hung up on the guy in spite of his gambling.' Peterman paused. 'That's how she seemed. And that's it, really. We started to chase down the Italian angle and then it blew up in our faces. Then Marinelli shifted Bardetski out of sight and told me you were going to take over. How we going to work it?'

'I don't know yet. It seems simple, doesn't it? Hunter owed the mob money. He went to pay them off but they killed him anyway. Why? Was he late? Was the killer acting a little independently? Did Hunter lose his cool and attack him? You could read that into the knife wounds: first the killer had to defend himself, then he strangled Hunter. Maybe a thousand wasn't enough? Maybe he owed them more and tried to bargain, so they made an example of him? You think there's much chance of finding him?'

'Not if it was one of those reasons. The hit man was probably from Michigan and he's back there now. Even if he's from the Toronto mob, you'd have to find him to make the forensic stuff any use.'

'The lab reported yet?'

Peterman nodded. 'They found some fibres of navy blue wool, probably from the killer's sweater.'

'Have you checked to see if the gambling squad have ever heard of Hunter?'

'I'll do that right away.'

'Hold on. Have you talked to Inspector Corelli?'

'Not that, either. I'll do that next.'

'I'll do it. I'll check them both. Something to do. Not too promising, is it?'

'Frankly, Staff, I'm glad you're taking over. You know why?'

'Sure. It's a very public case, and this reporter plans to make his name with it, but it's a mob thing, so when we get nowhere it'll be me he writes about.'

'That's it. We've had our share. You can have the rest.' Now Peterman was grinning.

'In the meantime, we don't have too many people to question, do we?' Salter was talking to himself. 'If I'm going to get nowhere, then I'd better be seen trying. Just for comfort's sake, I'll go over the ground you've covered—the clerk, Connie Spurling—and I'll check out Corelli and the gambling squad.'

'You want me along?'

'What for? Go and find those orientals who keep shooting each other. I'll let you know when I need both of us.'

'Great.' Peterman stood up, or rather, slid off the chair and balanced on his undersized feet. 'By the way, er, sir, I've got special plans for tonight and Saturday afternoon. If this thing blows up, naturally I'll be right there, but the critical time is over so I wondered, if it doesn't blow up, if I could count on those dates. Tonight and Saturday afternoon.'

Salter waited for the reasons. When Peterman said nothing more, he asked, 'Personal stuff?'

'That's right.'

'Very important?'

'It is to me.'

Why can't I know about it? Salter wondered. Marriage counselling, probably, the occupational pastime of policemen, but Peterman's acquaintance with Salter was too slight for him to want to share his problems.

'Sure,' Salter said. 'I'm just going to go through the motions, baby-sitting until this reporter goes away, then hand it over to the organized crime boys. Thanks for the warning. But you know better than me that I can't guarantee it.'

'I'll be on call. Thanks. By the way, watch out for Jack Huey, the reporter. Jensen played hockey against him in one of those friendly no-body-contact games when Huey was a political reporter up at Queen's Park. Huey was the dirtiest player on the ice.'

THREE

INSPECTOR CORELLI was the in-house specialist on organized crime. At one time the force had had a civilian, a graduate in criminology, whose job it had been to absorb all the available information on the ways of organized crime, in order, in his own words, 'to think mob thoughts' whenever a crime seemed to be linked to the organization. Budget cuts had eliminated him, and now the force relied on Corelli. Although, like Marinelli, his name suggested he might have an inside track, Corelli was a fair-haired descendant of a Northern Italian family that operated a truck garden forty miles north of Toronto. And like Marinelli, Corelli did not speak Italian.

Salter found him in his office and explained his mission.

'Yeah, Marinelli told me,' Corelli said immediately. 'Could be, of course. But the method sounds a little strange. Strange enough so it should help you to track him down. A knife? A ligature? Sure, they've used those, but nowadays a bullet behind the ear is the preferred method. This garrotting stuff—you read about it, mainly in those family novels about the mob, but I think it must have been popular because it was quiet. Nowadays, they use guns. I think any ligatures in the last ten years have been used by amateurs. But sure, a fancy mob killer who's seen too many movies or read too many books might want to try it. It might appeal as kind of—what? not stylish, but maybe craftsmanlike, done by hand, you know? If you've got that kind of mind.'

Salter said, 'You heard the uproar when someone said Italian?'

'I heard it, and I understood it. Bardetski's an asshole. "Fine Italian hand," for Chrissake. My daughter looked it up. It's nothing to do with killing. It's about handwriting.'

'Maybe that's what he meant. That the ligature was somebody's signature.'

'You can't blame us Italians for getting uptight.'

'What we have to do now is find a killer named Bushtinkle or Chow.'

'Until you do, it stays around as an unsolved Mafia killing.'

Salter said nothing. After a while Corelli continued, 'Otherwise, I guess it *is* the mob and we'll get it when the fuss has died down. So what can I do for you? Phone the godfather, ask him what the hell he's playing at?'

'Yeah.'

Corelli looked up sharply, then smiled. 'I already have. That is, I've called a guy who knows a man who's in touch with a lad who hears things and passes them on. The answer, so far, is negative. I've said I'm here if the information changes. See, a couple of times in the past, when there's been what looked like a gang killing, they sent a message that it wasn't them. Nobody actually phones Mackenzie and says, "Itsa notta us, boss," but *someone* gets a call, someone right outside the mob. There's a guy who runs a little dry-cleaner's shop on St Clair West who won't sell his business to them—I think it must tickle these characters to launder their money through dry-cleaners—and he won't contribute to the funds. Normally, he'd be out of business in a week, but they leave this guy there because he's useful to them for sending messages, like Switzerland during the war. They know he's honest, we know he's honest, so they can leave messages with him to pass on to us. You can't trust them, of course. The day we don't check, they'll set us up, so we're always looking for the reason behind it. But it is a message, better than nothing at all. There's a couple of other ways they like to get a word to us, and it works the other way. We know the families, and I can sometimes tap someone for information if our interests coincide. Of course, if I ask, "Who killed Cock Robin—You?" they always say no, but sometimes they add something that convinces us.'

'One time one of their soldiers was trying a little low-level muscling on his own, and he killed a bakery owner up on Dufferin with a bomb. By mistake, we think—he wanted to frighten the baker—but anyway, the way we saw it, it had to be the mob, and then we got a pretty strong message that we were wrong, so we held off rounding up all the known criminals and a couple of days later the body of a minor mobster was found up at the tracks in the meat-packing yards. We were both right, of course. He was one of them, but that day, as I say, he was working for himself. They don't like private enterprise.'

'Are you telling me this has nothing to do with the mob?'

'I'm telling you what I heard, and that I think it's probably good information.' Corelli sighed. 'But if I were you I'd ignore it. Sure it's the mob.'

'I'll be back.'

SERGEANT HORVARTH of the gambling squad had the kind of face that makes children smile. In an ordinary blue suit he looked as if he were off duty, that his regular costume should be a baggy set of pantaloons with a little propeller on his head and intermittent jets of water coming out of his ears. In his round pink-and-white face two bulging blue eyes looked out over a permanent gap-toothed grin. His fair hair was a tightly knotted rug of blond curls.

'Need a hand?' he asked when Salter appeared in front of his desk. Salter nodded, wondering if Horvarth would produce a dummy hand from his pocket and give it to him. Salter explained who he was and what he wanted, passing a picture of Alex Hunter across the desk.

'Take a seat, Staff.'

Salter lowered himself gingerly into the chair, half-suspecting a farting cushion.

Horvarth looked up. 'I've never seen him, but that doesn't mean anything. Where did you say they found him?'

'In a motel called Days 'R' Done down on the lake-shore. His girlfriend says he probably went there to pay a gambling debt.'

'Right. We all heard about this one. Did he take the money?'

'So she thinks.'

'Then why did they kill him?'

'That's question number two.'

'Question number one is who killed him, right? Off the top of my head, I'd say no one I know. I'd put my money on the mob. Did you try Inspector Corelli?'

'He's trying to tap his sources. Why do you think it was no one you know?'

'I've been on the squad for two years. I know every serious bookie in Toronto. I know everyone who runs an important game. My clients don't kill people.'

'What do they do when a guy doesn't pay up? Call in a collection agency?'

'No, not even that. They cut off his credit. That's enough. See, these guys, my clients, depend on trust. They allow one bad debt per customer, then they cross him off. If the debt is serious they might send a collector.'

'To break his legs?'

'No, to explain how embarrassing it's going to be when the collector appears at his office or his home or wherever.'

'You mean to tell me no one collects gambling debts in the old way any more?'

'My clients never did. What they sometimes do is sell the paper to a shark, and, yeah, *he* might get rough. But killing a guy is pointless unless you are trying to make an example of him. That's what the mob does. You'll be keeping an open mind, but I think you have to look outside the regular gamblers for this one. What does Corelli think?'

'He's not sure. But I think he'd like to hear that it wasn't the mob.'

'I guess I'm not, either, but it's very unlikely. Corelli is the expert, but I'd've thought it was more his territory than mine. Or it's some private thing, nothing to do with the regular crowd.' He picked the photograph off the desk, his blue eyes bulging further to register concentration.

Salter said, 'We know he gambled. Is there any way you could find out who he bet with? It might be a start.'

'I couldn't get anyone to stand up in court, but, yeah, I'll do the rounds. See if I can pick up anything. But I don't have to ask about the motel. You wouldn't see any of the people I know around there. That joint is strictly drugs and hookers. The guys I know send out for what they need in that line. But I'll ask around. You want to know what size of bet he made, how often, if he was all paid up?'

'Whatever.'

'I'll start out at the track. I was planning a run out tomorrow. I've got a tip on the seventh.'

Some of the early impression was diminishing, but Salter would still not have been very surprised if Horvarth had concealed a small electric shock in his parting handshake.

HE HAD one more call to make. Twice before he had been assisted by a former undercover officer in the drug squad. Constable Ranovic was still working on the squad, but no longer undercover. He had recently been promoted to sergeant.

Salter congratulated him. 'I had to take it,' Ranovic said. 'I have to think about the future.'

'Why?' On their first case together Ranovic had enjoyed himself posing as a street-vendor during a royal visit, keeping an eye on the real street-vendors who were believed to be planning a demonstration. Ranovic had a strong dramatic or playacting streak in him and he had been in his element selling souvenirs around Yorkville. Later, when Salter needed an undercover officer for an investigation of some sabotage on a movie lot, he had asked for Ranovic, and the young constable had emerged from the assignment slightly stage-struck, so that Salter had wondered if he might quit the police for a career in acting. He had always been essentially carefree, so this talk of the future was new to Salter.

'My girlfriend is pregnant.'

'What does that mean? No, I know what pregnant means. I mean, are you going to get married, join the rest of us?'

'*I'd* like to. She doesn't want to. She says the pregnancy is an accident. She's not ready to decide about marriage yet, and she doesn't want to give up her job.'

'What does she do?'

'She's an accountant. A CA.'

'An abortion, then?'

'Not that, either. She's pro-choice, but she wants this baby. It'll soon be too late for an abortion, anyway. No: she wants the baby; I want the baby. I want to get married; she doesn't want to commit herself.

Marriage is for life, she says, we have to make a commitment, she says, she's seen too many couples like us break up, she says, and what kind of an environment would that be to raise a child in? So in some way I haven't quite figured out yet, it's better if the kid has a single mother, more stable than having two parents who don't make it. And she doesn't want to give up her job.'

'Are you going to move out, so she can be single?'

'No, we're going to carry on living together, though I don't know how long we'll last. It's like we're into therapy. Every time we talk, which is like every day, new stuff comes out and the whole ball game changes. I have to keep telling myself that I want her, never mind the talk, that I want the kid, and that I want to get married, though that's more important to my grandmother than it is to me. I don't mind how long it takes to get to the church. I figure that if we live together long enough and have the kid, then she'll want to get married eventually just to simplify the bookkeeping.'

'How does this make you ambitious?'

'I have to have a career, see. I mean, there's no way I'm gonna be a whatdyacallit—a house-husband. But it's dicey, her being a CA and me just a constable. As sergeant, I'm on the move, like her, so when we're deciding what to do we'll have two careers to take into account, not just hers. I wish to hell we could just have the kid and I could work overtime to look after them both, but it isn't going to happen. Did you go through any of this?'

Salter shook his head. 'All we had to worry about was getting married in time so the relatives didn't count on their fingers when the first baby was born. It was simpler.'

And it was, in the beginning. Salter held back from telling Ranovic that the simplicity had evaporated for his generation, too, but the change had come much later. At the point when previous generations had settled into complaining or resigned middle age, the homes of his contemporaries had turned into debating societies as they tried to cope with the flood of psychological and sociological information that was newly sensitizing every human relationship, especially between husbands and wives, so that every word and gesture, especially of the males, was made the subject of interpretation and the source of new family rows. When Salter wondered if it wasn't just a new kind of nagging he got a lecture from Annie, his wife.

Now he explained what he wanted from Ranovic. 'There's no indication of any kind that Hunter was into drugs as a user. But I know that motel's been in the news, something to do with drug-dealing, so would you check to see if any of your pals have seen him?'

Ranovic took the picture from Salter. 'You're right about the motel. There's a lot of action there, not just drugs, but pimping, too. I'll ask the boys. Got any advice for me?'

'Yeah. Don't take any advice from people my age. We're a little bit jealous of your problems.'

Peterman was waiting for him in his office. Salter told him of the feelers he had put out to Inspector Corelli and Joe Horvarth and Ranovic.

'You going to see the motel clerk and the girl-friend?' Peterman asked.

'They're next. How is she?'

'She was in shock when I talked to her. I think when she comes round she'll be a handful. She assumed I was stupid. When are you going to talk to the clerk?'

'As soon as I can. What's his name?'

'Arbour. Claud Arbour.'

'I'll do it now.' Salter dialled the motel, established that Arbour was on duty, and told him to expect him.

'I'll come with you,' Peterman said. 'We should sift through the reservations, just in case.'

FOUR

ON THE WAY OUT Salter asked Peterman about the
motel.

'It was built forty or fifty years ago, before the
Gardiner Expressway went up. At the time, tourists,
salesmen, all the people coming up from the border
and Niagara came in on Highway 2 along the lake-
shore. Then the expressway went in and started to
dump everyone downtown. So you've got a few motels stranded along the shore. They get the odd tourist
who wanders off the Queen Elizabeth Way too soon,
but most of the traffic at Days 'R' Done is sex.
Quickies during the day and pimps at night. We've had
one shootout so far this year and a lot of complaints.'

'And drugs?'

'That's what the shootout was about. We'd staked
it out and these assholes decided to make a stand. But
it's only small-time dealers who are involved, the ones
who have to buy from the real wholesalers, who are
the mob.'

'What do you hope to find in the register?'

'Nothing. It's just procedure. I should have done it
already. I'll go through the book and find out who was
registered that night. They've got twelve rooms.
Probably six will be taken according to the register—
enough to keep the tax man quiet. Four of the six will
be untraceable. The other two will be legitimate tour-

ists or salesmen, probably also untraceable but maybe we can find one of them who was sitting at his window that night, couldn't sleep, decided to take some pictures of the night sky, and got a shot of the killer standing on the doorstep of the room across the courtyard with a sash cord in his hand.'

Salter laughed. 'But you have to cover it.'

'Procedure. That's about it. It's not even a real neighbourhood so there's no doors to knock on to ask about mysterious guys they might have noticed running around.'

They pulled into an area of unweeded gravel in front of the motel. 'How long will it take you?' Salter asked.

'I'll be through before you are.'

CLAUD ARBOUR was a small dark youth of about twenty with shining black hair carefully brushed out from the crown and shaped into a helmet. He recognized Peterman, and bounced on his toes, waiting to serve him.

Peterman introduced Salter and asked for the reservation list for the night of the homicide. Arbour had the information ready, a thin bundle of cards held with a rubber band. 'I thought you would want these,' he said. His movements were brisk and excited, as he turned from one to the other.

Salter said, 'Can I come back there while he's going through these cards?' He pointed to the space behind Arbour.

Arbour looked over his shoulder at his office. There were three chrome and plastic chairs, a filing cabinet and a desk, part of which served as a shelf to hold a packet of sugar, powdered milk, a teapot, and several packets of junk food. 'It's not very splendid,' he said, opening the door beside the counter to let Salter in. He placed a chair for Salter and sat down across from him.

'How long have you worked here?' Salter asked.

'About t'ree months. Since I came from Chicoutimi.' His accent was French.

'You like the work?'

'It's terrible.' Arbour crossed his legs tightly and grinned. 'Terrible,' he repeated. 'But I don't mind. It's something to do until I get a break.'

'What kind of break?' Salter asked, as he was clearly being invited to do.

'I am an artist. A writer-performer. I write my own songs and play on the guitar.' He pointed to an instrument case in the corner of the room. 'I am trying to get someone to hire me, or someone else to sing my songs. There is lots of time in this job to write. And lots of strange people to write about.' His eyes sparkled.

'I'll bet. Tell me about this guy who reserved the room. Did you get a good look at him?'

'Enough. A writer must practise to notice the peculiarities of different people. I am writing this song about all the people I have seen at Days'R'Done. Every verse is about someone different, and there's a chorus. So whenever I can, I tell a little story, make a verse, about the people who come here. I made up one yesterday about the lady who came for a room without any luggage. She waits all afternoon for her lover who never comes. But when she left she looked happy. Why was that? You see?'

'What did he look like?'

'Sorry. He was a little bit taller than you, slightly bigger across 'ere.' Arbour touched each of his shoulders. 'A long coat with a belt. I forget his trousers and shoes. Per'aps I din't see them. La moustache—moustache?—a thin, neat one. Black glasses with big sides and a grey cap of mackintosh like golfers wear.'

'Face?'

'Dark. He needed a bit of a shave. And gold in his teeth.'

'Whereabouts?'

'I remember some gold. Maybe one filling. He didn't say much but there was something gold when he spoke. In the front. On top, I think. His nose was nothing. Just a nose.'

'Shirt? Tie?'

'His coat was closed at the top.'

'His hands?'

'Gloves.' Arbour stopped, interested. 'That was strange. It wasn't cold.'

'You said he had an Italian accent.'

'That's 'ow I heard it.'

'What did he say?'

'You gotta room? I need a rooma fora one night.'

'Sounds like Chico Marx.'

Arbour shrugged. 'I don't know him. That's what I heard. He signed the card, gave me his money, and I never saw him again. It was quite busy that night.'

'What name did he use?'

Arbour pointed to the outer room where Peterman was going through the registrations. 'Rossano,' he said. 'J. Rossano.'

Peterman held up the card.

Salter continued. 'Did anyone else catch your eye that night?'

'There was plenty of action, cars coming and going, but not many came into the office. Some of our regulars pay by the week and they get lots of visitors.' Arbour looked owlish. He was enjoying himself.

'Girls?'

'Most of the regulars are girls.'

'You know them?'

'Sure, but they all left, or rather they 'aven't been back.'

'Did any of them deal drugs?'

Arbour shrugged. 'Sure, but they don't put "drug-dealer" on the card when they register.'

'You've been very helpful.' Salter stood up and walked to the counter. 'Ready, Sergeant?'

While they were waiting for Peterman to tidy up the registration cards and put a rubber band around them, Salter said to the clerk, 'You live here?'

'For the moment, but the owner is very pissed off with me. She doesn't like me to cooperate with the police. But I've saved enough to last a little while. I don't care about her.' He grinned.

'Let us know where we can find you. You know where you're going?'

'Certainly I will. I don't have an address yet, but I have the Sergeant's card. I'll give him a call.'

'Come into the office tomorrow and look at some pictures. Something may click.'

'HELPFUL KID, isn't he?' Peterman said in the car on the way back to College Street.

'He's a writer, he says. Training himself to be observant. He gave a good description.'

'He also hates the owner. You'd think they'd get along, because she's French too, but not from Chicoutimi, I guess. I talked to her. She runs a rooming-house on Sherbourne, which is also a brothel, like this place. The morality squad have charged her twice, but she got off both times. Now, though, someone has put the tax people on to her, and that kid will be a great help to them. She made a mistake hiring him. You notice how neat and clean he is? She stinks, literally, and he finds her disgusting. Literally, not morally. Where to, now?'

'I'm off to see the girlfriend. I have an appointment in her office at four.'

'You don't need me along for that, do you? Drop me at the office and I'll start checking these registrations.'

CONNIE SPURLING ran her business from a suite of offices on Yonge Street below Bloor. When Salter walked in he found himself in an outer office, which was also the reception area. A girl in her early twenties was sitting staring at the screen of a word-processor, crying.

'Miss Spurling?'

The girl shook her head, the tears streaming, and ran out of the room through a side door. Salter continued over to the door of an inner office. 'Miss Spurling?' he asked again, through the door.

For a moment, the woman behind the desk simply stared at him, questioning his appearance in her doorway. Then, apparently remembering, she stood up and flashed a smile of mechanical brilliance at him. Then, apparently remembering something else, she switched it off. 'I've been waiting for you,' she said. 'Let's get it over with.' She pointed to a chair in front of her desk.

Salter looked at his watch. 'We said four...'

'I know, I know, but I didn't realize how much I've got on.'

Salter settled himself into the chair and made a business of arranging himself while he looked at her and the office. Both, he thought, could be described as Hi-Tec. The walls were lined with factory shelving; the exposed heating ducts were enamelled red, the desk was a slab of rock supported by black two-inch piping. Only the lighting was not rediscovered: a dozen halogen lamps were clamped to the ceiling beams.

Connie Spurling was wearing fatigues of closely-woven sackcloth and a platinum-looking wristwatch. Her hair, face and hands had all been buffed and polished to such a high state of naturalness that she looked like a robot, a brilliant replica of a successful woman in her forties, whose only flaw was that she was flawless.

'Your girl seems a little upset,' Salter began.

'I've been reviewing her performance. She has difficulty accepting critcism.'

'Don't we all?' He thought of a little joke, a fictitious self-help book about learning to like abuse, and decided not to share it with Connie Spurling. 'Miss Spurling, would you mind repeating what you told Sergeant Peterman about the last time you saw Alec Hunter.'

'Alec left after dinner, about seven-thirty. He was going to visit his great-aunt as he usually did on Sundays.'

'Fond of her, was he?'

'He was a dutiful nephew. The only one.'

'You gave him some money, Sergeant Peterman says.'

'The day before. A thousand dollars. Next I heard that the police had found him dead in the motel room.'

'What's the address of his great-aunt's institution?'

'It's called St. Bartholomew's. It's a converted mansion on Lowther. I don't know the number.'

'And that's the last you heard?'

'Until the police told me the next morning.' It was impossible to find the grief behind the words. She seemed to Salter now like something out of *Star Trek*, a creature from Noma, the one in the different-coloured jump suit who was really just an aura left behind by someone who had died four million years ago. 'He told you the money was for a gambling debt, did he?' Salter asked.

A flash of nerve ran along the jawbone, a flicker of emotion.

'He promised it would be the last one.'

Another nerve jumped in her cheek. Salter realized she was in the grip of very intense emotion, the signs shielded by her carefully held exterior. 'Can you tell me about these debts? How long have you been paying the bills?'

'About six or eight months, since the middle of August last year. Before that he had always kept them from me, but he eventually got into more trouble than he could manage.'

'How much in all did you give him?'

'Ten or eleven thousand. Sometimes a thousand, sometimes two, every three or four weeks.'

'Why? Why did you keep on? Did you try to get him to stop?'

'For God's sake, of course I did. And I was sure that he had finally got up the willpower, so one last thousand and that was that. Anyway, what has this got to do with how he was killed?'

Not much, Salter admitted silently. Just curious. 'Did he ever say anything about the person he had to pay?'

'A bookie. That's all I know.'

'Did he have friends he might have talked to about it?'

'I wouldn't think so. He didn't have any real cronies. You could talk to Bill Turgeon, the stage manager. He and Alec were as near buddies as Alec had.'

'Did he have any women friends, apart from you?'

'Did someone tell you to ask that?' Her tone was intended to draw blood.

Salter waited before he replied to register that he had heard the tone and saw that it was intended to provoke him. 'You're the first person I've spoken to who knew him,' he said.

'When you do speak to his acquaintances you'll find out that there were no other women. When I took Alec over, not just as his agent, it was on condition that he drop all the others. And I think he did.'

Salter said, 'The play he was in before he died. It's still on, isn't it?'

'He was the lead in *After Paris*, but he left it the week before he was killed. The play is still on because the understudies have taken over.'

'Why did he quit?'

'He didn't "quit". He only accepted a three-month contract in the first place because he was committed to go to Vancouver next week to start work on a film. As it happens the film fell through, so he was free.'

'Was the play successful?' Salter had trouble finding the right term. A hit? A smasheroo?

'He got terrific reviews. Finally he was making a name. He'd waited so *long*.' She nearly shouted the last word. 'Five years of doing everything, but finally he's talked about. Then someone kills him.'

Salter said, 'I'm surprised. He was close to forty. What did he do before this last five years?'

'Everything and nothing. But in the last five years he was starting to get parts. I would have moved him.'

'Where is the play on?'

'The same place. The Estragon Theatre. I wouldn't bother, though. Alec held the whole thing together.

The schmuck they've got now couldn't play Santa Claus.'

'Still, I have to talk to whoever knew him. We're working in the dark so far.'

'You'll stay there, won't you? You never solve Mafia killings.'

'Where is the theatre?'

'Off Egerton Street. Between Bathurst and Spadina, north of Queen. Take my advice. Talk to Bill Turgeon. The others will only badmouth him. You see, Alec had talent.' She executed the classic file-shuffling gesture. 'Now, if you don't mind, I have to work.'

Salter was tempted to invent ten more questions to show who was in charge around here, but then he remembered that she was entitled to her own reaction to her grief, and he left.

THE CRYING GIRL was waiting for him outside the building, holding her coat close to her throat as if she was cold. Her nose was cherry red. 'Excuse me,' she said. 'You're a policeman, aren't you? An inspector or something. Could I talk to you?'

'Sure. What about?' This was in half the movies. She would now tell him about a man with an Italian accent who had visited Connie Spurling the day before Hunter's death, and of the argument she had overheard, which had ended when Connie Spurling had sent the girl to the bank to cash a cheque for five thousand dollars.

'Could we go somewhere else?' the girl asked. 'She might come out.'

'Over there.' He pointed to a café across the street.

In the café he ordered coffee for both of them and waited for the revelations. When the girl tried to sip hers, her teeth rattled slightly against the cup. She put it down quickly and pulled a cigarette from her bag. 'Do you mind?' Getting a shrug from Salter, she lit up.

'This is silly,' she said. 'But I'm terrified of her. I'm not going back. Is there anything she can do to me?'

'Like what? Do you have pay coming?'

'She can keep it. I mean, she might accuse me of stealing something.'

'Is she that bad?'

'She's *unbelievable*. I've been here a month, and look at me.'

'What, exactly, did she do to you today?'

'She *assessed* me. I thought I was doing so well, then before you came, she had me in for my assessment. *Three pages* of faults and not a single positive thing. I asked her, wasn't there anything good to say, and if not, why didn't she fire me the first week, and she said that wasn't the purpose of the assessment which was to see my weaknesses and get me to improve on them. I said, couldn't she just *tell* me my strengths, just so I would know, but she wouldn't. God, she was so *destructive*. So I asked her if she was going to fire me, and she said that was typical negativism on my part.' The girl began to cry again. 'Nobody will believe me. I'll look like a total failure.'

'But you've quit. She didn't fire you. You have quit, haven't you?'

'Of course. I can't stand it. For the first three weeks she was as sweet as pie and then she started finding fault. Then today she let me have it. I'm sure it's why the last girl left.'

'Maybe it's some kind of management technique.'

'I'm sure it is. She didn't get angry. She went into everything—my attitude, as she called it—I mean, that's who I am, right?—the way I look—my unwillingness to make an extra effort—that's because I had tickets to *The Phantom* when she wanted me to work all night. She left me with this big pile of work and went off to a dinner-party. *God.*'

'She's been under a lot of strain. It's quite a thing having your boyfriend murdered.'

'This has been going on for *weeks*. I tried to say something sympathetic, but she told me to shut up. I don't think that's got anything to do with it. I think she just likes *assessing* people.'

'Didn't the news affect her much?'

'It must have, but how could you tell? She was obsessed with him. She told me if he called when she was out, I had to let her know wherever she was. *Imagine.* And if she was in the office and I answered when he called she acted as if I had no business picking up the phone. She even came out of her office to make sure I wasn't listening in. He came to the office one day— just once—and I didn't know who he was, and he was chatting me up and I was trying to be all sparkly with a client as she said I should, and she came out of her office and cut me off in mid-sentence. Obsessive, possessive, you name it.'

'She never said anything to you about his death?'

'To me? Never. As far as her personal life was concerned, I didn't exist. I wasn't even allowed to say she looked nice, as if I was some kind of servant. It was a shock, though. After the two policemen had gone, I went in to see if there was any trouble I could help with. She just said that Alec Hunter was dead; he'd been killed by gamblers. I said how did she know who killed him, and she said because he said that's what would happen but she didn't believe him. Then she told me to get on with my work.'

The girl was relaxing fractionally. Salter had learned something, but he was unlikely to learn anything more. 'So what do you want me to do?'

'You're a policeman, right?' She put her large leather bag on the table, and shook out the contents. 'Office shoes, rest-of-my-lunch, Kleenex, book, *Mademoiselle*, wallet, scarf, change purse.' She upended the bag to show it was empty. 'There. Could I tell them you inspected my bag?'

'Who?'

'If anyone accuses me.'

'Are you serious?'

'You don't know what she's like! If she finds a floppy disc missing in two years' time she'll accuse me. I know.'

It was serious enough, Salter understood, not the reality but the fact that the girl could imagine it. 'What do you want me to do? Give you a note, like?' He smiled, trying to make light of it.

'Something,' she said.

'Here. Here's my card. If the cops arrive, show them this and have them phone me. And give me a number where I can reach you. In the meantime you'd better call her and tell her you're not coming back.'

'Tomorrow. I can't deal with her today.'

WHILE ANNIE WAS AWAY, Salter and his younger son had quickly fallen into a routine, not of cooking supper together, but of letting each other know if they were going to be home at supper-time. If they were, Salter called on his repertoire of bacon and eggs and steaks and microwaved potatoes, but in the five days Annie had been gone, they had only managed it twice. Now Salter called home but Seth was out, busy rehearsing a play he was in, a semi-professional production of *The Monkey's Paw* to be put on at a lunchtime theatre. Salter told his answering machine he would not be home until late, and there was some money in the bowl on the top shelf of the kitchen cupboard that it could use to buy itself supper. Then he went in search of Peterman.

'The kid from the motel was in, on his way home,' Peterman said. 'I took him right through the roster, showed him all the pictures, even pressed him a little bit when we came to anyone who we think is working for the mob, especially anyone with a gold tooth. Nothing. He's a good witness if we do find a suspect, because he wasn't about to finger someone just to please me.'

'So it's someone we don't have on file. Are there many of those, do you think?'

Peterman looked as if it were the kind of question he would expect from a television host on a chat show about rising crime in Metro, not from a professional policeman. 'There are some here in town, I would think,' he said. 'They come and go. There's probably about a hundred in Buffalo, and about the same in Detroit. Niagara Falls, New York, would have about twelve.'

Salter caught the tone, or rather the absence of tone, the note of wonder that shouted irony, and had to force himself to remember what question of his Peterman was answering. Now the look on Peterman's face seemed to suggest that Salter had been babbling out loud. Salter decided to take it on. 'Sorry,' he said. 'My wife's away, her father's had a stroke, and I was just calling home to leave some messages for my kid.'

But the real reason was that the lilacs had come back, and with them the sense that all this was piddling and irrelevant, and he could be thinking about something serious like deciding exactly how he wanted to spend the next and last twenty years of his life, instead of pretending to pursue some gorilla with a gold tooth who was almost certainly right then counting his killing fee in a Detroit hotel room.

Peterman nodded. 'You seemed kind of out of it,' he agreed, and Salter could tell from his voice that he had lost a little bit of Peterman, and he had better work to get it back.

'There's nothing in the motel registrations,' Peterman continued. 'Garbage. Only one of them looks real, a guy from Arizona, probably a tourist, by now probably in Alaska. His room wasn't close, so he isn't worth chasing down.'

'Did you check out this old folks' home where Hunter was supposed to be the night he was killed?'

For the first time in their short acquaintance, Peterman looked uncomfortable. 'I called them. They said he had been to see his great-aunt that night.'

'For how long?'

'They didn't say.'

'I'll go and talk to them,' Salter said.

'I couldn't see that it mattered a hell of a lot. That was his excuse to Connie Spurling. So he called in on his great-aunt first, then went to the motel.'

'It's a detail. If we know what time he left the home we know when he might have got to the motel.'

'And?'

Salter nodded. 'And nothing, probably. But the other thing is, if he went to see her first, then it doesn't sound as if he was geared up for a big confrontation.'

'Just your usual Sunday night. Go see Great-aunt Jemima, then deliver a thousand to some hood.'

'Sounds like it. I'll talk to them anyway.' It was something to do.

WHEN HE RANG THE BELL at St Bartholomew's, the face of an elderly woman stared at him through the glass front door. Another face, this time of a middle-aged woman, appeared beside the first, and the door opened.

Salter showed his identification and stepped around the old lady who stood unmoving in his way. Her eyes slid round to watch Salter go by, but she remained

facing the front door. Beyond the entrance was a
lounge area. The middle-aged woman closed the door
and touched his arm. 'Let's go into my office. Not
you, Doris, you come and drink your tea.' She turned
the old lady around and walked her to an armchair
and sat her down in front of a half-empty cup of tea.
'See? You haven't finished it yet. You've been too busy
with the door.'

The lounge was empty except for a very old man
who was sitting in a corner, staring at the wall. As
Salter watched, the man slowly raised a hand and
moved it in the direction of his face, but before he
could complete the movement, his other hand fell off
the arm of the chair, distracting him, leaving him
staring at his dangling left hand, his right hand still
raised near his chin.

So this is it, Salter thought. Ending up. This is
probably how Annie's father looks. He saw now what
his mother-in-law was afraid of and why she wanted
to stay home surrounded by dependent offspring,
awaiting the day when she would need someone to put
her hand back on the arm of the chair, and he felt
some sympathy without in any way wanting to offer
himself as the solution to her fears.

The supervisor came back to Salter now and led him
along the hall. 'Doris is a funny old duck sometimes,'
she said. 'We have quite a few funny old ducks here.
I'm Nora Halbird, the day manager.'

Salter said, 'Looks nice. Very nice. Comfortable.
People look very calm.'

'The one you saw, the old chap, has Alzheimer's.'

'Ah.'

'You're here about Mrs Heliwell.'

'Alec Hunter's great-aunt.'

'That's her. I read all about him. What can I tell you?'

'I believe he was here last Sunday night.'

'I wasn't on duty. Susan was the night nurse. I can get her on the phone. I was just talking to her. Hang on a moment.' She got up quickly and moved past Salter to an old lady in the hall who had become entangled in her four-legged walker. Mrs Halbird got the lady's hands in the proper places, pointed her in the right direction and waited while she took the first steps down the corridor.

When she returned she saw the look on Salter's face and smiled. 'Think of it as a kindergarten,' she said. 'And imagine what it's like in the winter, getting them dressed properly for a little walk.'

'I guess somebody's got to do it,' Salter said.

'That's how you see it? I suppose so. For me it's just an interesting job, more useful than most, but I'm not sacrificing myself. Now where were we?'

In some way, Salter felt himself admonished, as if he had been sympathizing with a prison guard only to find that the guard was on the side of the inmates. 'You were talking about the night nurse,' he reminded her.

'Right. I'll call her now.'

A minute later the night nurse was on the line. 'Yes, he was. He came around eight. I let him in, but he found his own way up to her room. He's been often enough.'

'When did he leave?'

'I don't know. I'm pretty sure he didn't leave before nine-thirty because I was in the lounge all the time until nine, then I did the rounds before I served tea, which takes until about nine-thirty. He must have left when I was in the office, between about nine forty-five and ten-thirty. Somebody must have let him out. He came every Sunday so I didn't check up on him.'

Salter heard the note of worry in her voice. Security, to prevent people wandering out into the street, would be important in a place like this. He thanked her and hung up, turning back to Nora Halbird. 'Why would someone have to let him out?'

'It's a little system we have. You can let yourself out with a key, but if you don't have a key someone has to press a buzzer while you open the door. You can't do both things yourself. We tread a fine line between keeping an eye on them and not making them feel they are under guard.'

'Someone let him out, then?'

'Someone pressed the buzzer, but I wouldn't bother trying to ask them to remember who it was.' She smiled. 'They wouldn't make very good witnesses in court.'

'Did you know Alec Hunter?'

'I met him lots of times. If one of the nurses has a date, I'll do the evening part of her shift, and then I'll get a morning from her some time. Yes, I met Mr Hunter.'

'He was pretty faithful? Visiting her?'

'Ever since her daughter died. His aunt, that was.'

Salter waited for more.

'He was now her only relative, her heir. This place costs two thousand a month, which the lawyer pays out of the interest on her capital. The rent of two houses she owns, actually. But, at least she got a visitor. Some of these people don't even get visited on their birthdays.'

'Can I meet her?' Salter asked.

'Sure.'

She took him along the hall to a small elevator. Inside the elevator, another old lady was waiting for the door to close. When she saw them about to get in she scrambled out and waited in the hall, staring at them in distress.

'We'll be right back, Jennie,' Halbird said soothingly.

They got in and the door closed. 'Jennie will not ride with anyone else,' Halbird said. 'She gets frightened in such a small space.'

'It *is* a pretty enclosed space,' Salter said, holding his breath to cut down on body contact.

Mrs Heliwell was watching television with her door open. Nora Halbird switched it off and tried to introduce Salter.

'Leave me alone,' the old lady shouted. She looked at Salter. 'They've been beating me all night. *And* throwing cold water over me. I'm black and blue and frozen. It's disgusting.'

Halbird switched the set back on and led Salter back to the elevator. 'She's having a bad day. If you want her to talk sense, you'll have to come back.'

'What was that all about?'

'On her bad days, she can't tell the difference between dreaming and waking. She must have had a nightmare last night and she's still in it. The nurse reported that she was shouting half the night.'

'She looks pretty strong, though.'

'She could live forever. It doesn't matter now, but when Mr Hunter was around I sort of hoped she would. It was pretty obvious where his interests lay. He tried to get power of attorney but the lawyer stopped that. But now I've said too much. I'm just supposed to keep them all comfortable, that's all. Anything else I can tell you?'

'All I need to know is that he came here on Sunday.'

'He did that.' She pressed the buzzer and Salter let himself out.

THE FOLLOWING MORNING Salter went in search of Sergeant Horvarth of the gambling squad to see what the sergeant had dug up for him. He found Horvarth's possessions stacked in his Out-tray. His colleague, Sergeant Lindstrom, told him that Horvarth had been sent on leave.

'What does that mean?'

'I don't know. They told me when I came in this morning. As far as I know, he had no plans. I called him at home, but he just shut down like there was someone with a gun in his back. "I'm on leave," was all he said, and hung up.'

Salter took Horvarth's home number and returned to his office to call him.

At first, Horvarth repeated his statement. Then, when Salter did not go away, he said, 'Didn't they tell you? I'm under investigation. On the take, they think. I've been asked to say nothing, and that's what I plan to do, but you and the deputy seem to be pals so you'll hear anyway. Even the squad doesn't know.' Horvarth's voice was tight and angry, and Salter tried to imagine such a voice coming from the face of the happy clown.

'Do they have evidence?'

'They think they've got me red-handed.'

'Do they?'

'I'm reserving my defence, as they say. I don't know you, do I?'

'But you've got a defence?'

Horvarth stayed silent.

'Have you?'

Horvarth said, 'Staff Inspector, I don't want to sound—what's the word, insubordinate?—but I've been accused of taking money. That's serious. So when I say I'm reserving my defence, I mean that right now, until I find out what's going on, I'm assuming that I'm on my own, and that you, for instance, are speaking for the deputy.'

Salter said, 'I haven't seen the deputy this morning. I got the news when I came to look for you. They told me you were on leave.'

'Uh-huh.'

Salter said, 'I might as well ask you anyway. Before this happened, did you find out anything for me?'

'You can't trust me now, of course, but I'll tell you I only just had time to put the question out. The answers will come in over the next couple of days, but I won't be there to hear them, will I?'

'Shall I go back to Lindstrom, then? Ask him to do it? You're the guy with all the contacts, I was told.'

'Problem, isn't it?'

Salter waited.

'Ah, shit, you aren't trying to screw me, I guess. I'll put the word out again and have them call you. OK?'

'Thanks.' Salter put the phone down, wondering. Before he moved on to Corelli, he decided to call on the deputy.

'CLOSE THE DOOR, Salter.' The deputy ran a hand over one of the last crew-cuts on the force. 'I know what you're here for. Horvarth. We've got pictures. A bookie, a known bookie, handing over a bundle of notes to him in a parking lot.'

'Who took them?'

'The Mounties.'

'Jesus.' Salter sat down opposite the deputy.

'Nice, eh? And all the new politicians in their white hats.'

Salter said, 'Has there ever been anything like this about him before?'

'Not while I've been deputy.'

'I was just talking to him on the phone. He didn't sound like a guy who was worried his career was finished. He sounded angry as hell. I'd be a little wary, sir.'

The deputy nodded four or five times. 'I know. I think he's acting very strange. When I told him that there was evidence that he had taken money, he

wanted to know what it was. I didn't tell him. He
wanted to know who collected the evidence. I can't tell
him that. Not yet. So he just said fine, and shut up.
Now I'm trying to decide what to do.'

'The Police Act? Or a criminal charge?'

'I have to hold an internal inquiry under the rules.
Then charge him under the act or the criminal code.'
He looked out the window. 'Ten years ago, I know
what I'd've done. I'd've settled it first, right in here,
before I went public. That way you don't get any surprises when you hold the inquiry, and you sometimes
don't have to hold it at all. But things are getting very
official. If I did that now and the word got out,
someone would start screaming cover-up, and I'd have
the commission to deal with. But I agree with you.
Horvarth's looking for blood, though how the hell he
can beat this, I don't know. What possible defence has
he got?'

'That's for him to know and you to find out, is what
I heard.'

'I've got to do something, Salter. The Mounties are
feeling very self-righteous about this.'

'You've sent Horvarth on leave. He isn't saying a
word. Take a couple of days, and maybe he'll tell you
himself, then you'll know what to do. You might be
able to go back ten years.'

'He's up to something, isn't he?'

'He's got some kind of answer.'

The deputy looked at Salter from under his eyebrows. 'You think he might tell you what he's up to?
You two don't have a history, do you?'

Salter could see how much Mackenzie hated the position he was in, wanting to avoid a public inquiry enough to admit that Salter might be able to do his job for him.

'Can it wait, sir? Horvarth has just taken up his position. Tomorrow he might not be so happy in it.'

'Use your own judgement, Salter. I'll tell you when I have to move.'

INSPECTOR CORELLI SAID, 'The word I've got is that it isn't the mob. If it isn't, I'm sure we'll get a sign. They don't like unnecessary publicity.'

'I'll still hold it as the main possibility.'

'Yeah, I would, if I were you. You have to. I'd start looking elsewhere, too, though.'

This wasn't very good news. Salter would not have been unhappy to learn that the mob had already executed their man who had stepped out of line, so that he could think about more important things.

After his visit to the old folks' home he had had an urge to visit his own father who was now well into his seventies, and seemed content enough living with the widow of an old friend. But even as he experienced the thought, he knew that so long as his father was in his right mind he would treat any sudden change in his son's concern for him with intense suspicion. Nevertheless, he could not help wondering what the future held for the old man, and for himself. Following that thought, and thinking about the way his mind was working, Salter began to wonder if he was going through a crisis, a change from which he would suddenly wake up, aged. Against all the jaunty bloom of

the men who claimed they felt ten years younger now
that they were retired he put the image of one in his
early sixties who became an old man within a year of
retirement, shuffling about with a soft smile on his
face. He comforted himself by thinking about his
genes. His own father at seventy had moved in with
the widow and made it clear with a dozen winks and
nods that he was enjoying full connubial bliss. So that
was all right. Then why couldn't he forget it?

NEXT HE CHECKED with Ranovic on the drug squad's
reaction.

'We don't know him,' Ranovic said. 'That means he
isn't a regular dealer.'

'Thanks. I'd have been surprised if you did. I
haven't picked up a whisper about drugs. I was just
checking.' He got up to leave. 'What's happened on
the home front?'

'It's worse. We've agreed on everything except getting married. She's going to have the baby, we're getting a Filipino nanny—that's what everyone does
now—and she and I will carry on just like before. The
only thing is, she wants the two of us to buy a house
in the Brown school district.'

'Why?'

'Brown school has a French immersion programme.'

'They don't take them at birth, do they?'

'No, but she's planning ahead. She thinks it's very
important that our kid knows both official lan-
guages.'

'By the time your kid goes to school, Quebec will have separated. Ontario's other official language will be Italian. Better look for a place on St Clair West.'

'We talked about that. She thinks that French will be even more important then, that there'll be a big demand for professionals who can operate in both countries. Frankly I'm a little pissed off with it all. In my house the other official language will be Croatian. I'm going to talk Croatian exclusively while I'm alone with the kid.'

'Your Croatian still good?'

'Not very.' Ranovic grinned. 'My father wouldn't allow it to be spoken when I was growing up so us kids would be thoroughly Canadian. I'm going to take lessons. My brother, by the way, is married to a Portuguese girl who's gotten very gung-ho about *her* heritage, so his kids have to learn Portuguese which my mother doesn't like much. My brother doesn't care but my mother goes to visit and overhears her grandchildren talking to her son in broken Portuguese—on Sundays the rule is only Portuguese—and then she starts a fight with her daughter-in-law.'

'In English.'

'More or less.'

'So you are going to raise your kid speaking English, French and Croatian?'

'And Filipino. Don't forget the Nanny.'

'Jesus. But you're not going to get married.'

'What she says is that if we get married, society will put pressure on her to be the caring parent—this is her talking—which means stay home, look after the kid. She says she read in a magazine that there's a new conservatism encouraging wives to play their traditional role and she's not having any part of it. She says that social pressure-wise it's going to be easier to be a single mother than a separated wife. If the relationship doesn't work, that is. You know, she's looking forward to this kid like you wouldn't believe—she's already talking to her belly when she thinks no one is around—but her head is full of this other thing. It sure as hell was a lot easier for your generation, wasn't it? I mean, you met someone, got her pregnant and you got married. Right?'

'Hey!'

'I don't mean you personally. I mean your generation. Most of you didn't have sex until you got married, or just before, did you?' Ranovic looked at him inquisitively.

'I think you're talking about Ireland. We had Millie. We used to meet her in the garage after school on Fridays.'

'Yeah?'

'You're never going to know, Gorgi. But keep me in touch. I hope I'm still around for the wedding.'

'You're at the top of the list. Sorry I couldn't help with this guy. By the way, wasn't he in the movie we were involved with last summer?'

'I thought I'd said that. He was one of those two guys who tried to beat up the hero. We did the scene behind that warehouse on King Street.'

'Maybe I should check around with the people who knew him on the set. Derek or Neville might know him.' Ranovic named the two make-up men whose truck he had driven.

'You still in touch with them?'

Ranovic looked embarrassed. 'Mason Stone made a movie here in town, in Chinatown, and Derek and Neville let me hang around the make-up truck.'

'Have you got yourself a union card yet?'

Ranovic said, 'I'm about to be a family man. I need a regular income.'

Salter suppressed the impulse to make any more jokes. Ranovic clearly had not recovered from being slightly stage-struck, and he might be too vulnerable to being teased. 'So ask them. Find out anything you can about this guy. Find out about his gambling, or his women. Anything they know about Connie Spurling. Did the guy have any enemies they know of? Anything at all.'

SIX

THE BOOKIE CALLED early in the afternoon. His name was Maurice Taber. His message was simple. He had never heard of Hunter, and no one he knew had, either. He could not guarantee, however, that Hunter was not known at the level of people who killed clients who did not pay up. He was not familiar with that world himself. 'Of course,' he added, 'I'm retired. He may have come on the scene very recently.'

'When did you retire, Mr. Taber?'

Taber ignored the question. 'Anything else?' he asked. 'I'd like to help, if only as a favour to a friend.'

'Who's the friend?'

'Joe Horvarth. I hear he's been sent on leave. You people are as stupid as most of my old clients, you know that?'

Salter had a sudden urge to meet this man. 'You have time on your hands, Mr. Taber? Now that you're retired? I'd like to know how your old world works. Can I buy you a drink?'

'I often spend a little time in the bar of the Mercury Hotel. About four blocks from you. I'll be there about four. Any use to you?'

'I'll drop by.'

THE BAR of the Mercury Hotel was large, dark, and at four o'clock, not very busy. Each of about twenty tables was ringed by four chairs. The bar was along one side, running for about a third of the length of the room. A row of booths filled the rest of the wall. Salter took a table near the wall on the opposite side to the booths. Within a few minutes he had identified Taber as the man in the back booth who was being consulted from time to time by one of the waiters. As Salter watched, he saw that the consultations were preceded by phone calls the waiter took at the bar. Taber seemed to have come out of retirement since that morning.

Salter called a waiter over to ask him if he knew of a Mr Taber, and watched him speak to Taber's waiter who consulted Taber who send a nod down the line to Salter who moved across the room, leaving his beer to be brought by the waiter in obedience to an old Ontario law that makes it illegal to be upright and moving in public while holding an alcoholic beverage.

Maurice Taber was a well-dressed and groomed man in his mid-forties, with flat fair hair like Fred Astaire. As Salter sat down, Taber said to the waiter, 'I want to talk to the police inspector without any interruptions.'

The waiter nodded in a huge arc and looked to left and right in case anyone was approaching whom he might have to kill. Salter thought that Taber's tips must be something special.

'I don't know how much help I can be,' Taber began. 'I've never heard of this man—Hunter, was it?'

In going to meet a bookie, Salter had assumed there would be some hint of Damon Runyon. At the very least, a cigar. But Maurice Taber looked like a successful practitioner of one of the minor healing arts, one that required to be well-manicured. A chiropodist, or a dentist.

Salter nodded. 'What does that mean? The fact that you've never heard of him.'

'For one thing, it means he never went to Woodbine racetrack. Have you found anyone else who knows him?'

'You're the first response I've had.'

'Nobody I know has heard of him.'

'You did say there were people you didn't mix with.'

'I've put out some more feelers since this morning. I don't think he's known. Nobody knows him. I'd've heard.'

'In which case?'

'In which case he probably dealt with the mob. Do you know how much was involved?'

Salter told him.

Taber shook his head, surprised. 'Chickenfeed for them. Not worth killing anyone for, I would think. But then, I stay a million miles away from those babies.'

'Somebody killed him, Mr Taber. Somebody connected with gambling.'

'Yes. I thought it would be worth coming out of retirement to tell you that it wasn't one of us. We work on trust. We forget about bad debts, but we don't trust them again. If you want my opinion, this man Hunter was not into gambling of the kind I used to know, not around Toronto.'

'My sources are pretty definite on the subject.'

'So are mine. If I hear anything different I'll let you know. But that isn't really why I came down here this afternoon.'

Salter looked over his shoulder at the waiter standing by the bar. 'From what I can see, you came down to keep your hand in.'

Taber crooked a finger at the waiter, who came over and filled his coffee cup. 'Are you still investigating Joe Horvarth?' he asked.

'What are you talking about? He started to help me, then went on leave.'

'He's the subject of an investigation for taking bribes, I hear.'

'You're got big ears, Mr Taber.'

'He called me, remember, to ask me to help you.'

'Ah.' Salter nodded, acknowledging Taber's right to ask questions.

'So what's he supposed to have done?'

'You just told me, taking money.'

'How was he caught?'

'We'll all hear, one day.'

'Then I'll tell you something . . .'

' . . . this is like getting messages from the mob . . .'

' . . . Whoever is accusing Horvarth—your boss—has got his head up his ass, a long way up. Joe is the best man you've got, or used to have—he's no use to anyone now. He's arrested me twice, and that's about the average for everyone he keeps tabs on. He has never laid himself open to pay-offs. The odd drink around the fire, as it were, but never serious money. The fact is that Joe has nothing against betting—he bets himself—but it was his job to keep it from getting out of control, which he was very good at doing. It was a matter of pride with him to keep a tight lid on the game. If he could catch us taking serious bets, setting up a card-room, fleecing Shriners, anything like that, he would. If he couldn't, then no one else could either, so it was under control, he was doing his job. But there was nothing personal about the way he operated. We knew him, he knew us, and he tried to catch us if he could. I liked the guy. I could trust him, d'you see?'

'To do what?'

'Not to set me up. No entrapment. He was honest. We've all tried waving cabbage under his nose, but you only try once with him. He even allowed it—one free try. Knowing he wasn't on the take worked for us, too. Do I have to spell it out? Horvarth was, is, honest.' Taber looked away from Salter and nodded slightly to ready the waiter, a signal that he had told Salter everything he had come to say.

'OK. Thanks for the message. I'll take it back. But as you said, we can't trust it. It's what you'd say to protect a cop who was on the take, one you don't want replaced. But supposing it's on the level? Why are you telling me? What do you care? You like him that much?'

'I like to know where I stand, and with Horvarth I do. Now, can I buy you a drink?'

'I'll have a Tequila Sunrise, just so the waiter will remember me when they investigate me.'

Finally Taber smiled.

THERE WAS JUST TIME to catch the deputy before he
went home. Salter reported the conversation he had
had with Taber about Horvarth.

'Like you say, it cuts both ways, doesn't it?' Mackenzie said. 'Either they're trying to help Horvarth because he's honest and he's played square with them, or
they're trying to help him out because he isn't. What
do you think?'

'My feeling is that if Taber thought Horvarth had
been caught on the take, he'd just forget about him.
If I had to bet, I'd say that Taber is telling it straight.'

'Then what the hell is Horvarth up to? Look at this.'
He opened a drawer and took out a photograph.
Horvarth and an unknown man were standing in a
parking lot exchanging what was obviously a bundle
of money.

'Maybe Horvarth never took it. You can't tell in
that picture. He could even be giving it back.'

'The photographer thought of that.' The deputy
held up a stack of pictures. 'He took so many shots,
you could staple them together and make a movie.
Horvarth took the money and put it into his inside
coat pocket, then shook hands.'

After a while, Salter said, 'There isn't much you can
do, is there?'

'Maybe not, but it goes against the grain. You know
the most important lesson that a young cop has to
learn is, "Never ask a question if you don't know the
answer." That way you don't get any surprises, and
you know when someone is a liar. I don't like not
knowing what Horvarth is going to say when we ask
him.' He looked at Salter inquiringly.

Salter shook his head. 'I haven't tried to talk to him yet.' He could see what was coming and he wanted to do it in his own time.

But it was the wrong answer. 'Would you go out and talk to him? I need an objective opinion.'

'What do you want to know, exactly?'

'From him: what the fuck he's up to. From you: the same thing, about him. And finally, whether I can risk having a little informal inquiry before I go public. Get everybody in here for a chat to see what we've got.'

'Mounties, too?'

'If I can.'

'I'll try. I guess if I tell him it's my idea, then he won't scream that his right to a public hearing is being affected.'

'That's the spirit. Soon as you can, eh, Salter?'

AND THEN, walking through College Park Shopping Centre, on his way to a corned beef sandwich at the Pickle Barrel, he saw Julie Peters, the missionary's daughter.

At first he did not recognize her. He saw a woman in her early fifties: short chestnut hair with some grey; blue eyes and a very slightly tanned face without make-up, or with a superbly applied varnish (Salter had been fooled before). But the pinkish lipstick nibbled around the edges was the clue; she had no other make-up. The face, then: deep, pleasant lines, a soft face; then a dark red silky-looking suit over a creamy-coloured blouse; red leather shoes. Nice, he thought.

She was standing near the doorway of the bookstore, thumbing through a 'where-to-go-in-Toronto'

guide. Safe behind his own magazine, Salter fanta-
sized suggesting that he knew of a place. Then the first
layer peeled away and he realized she looked familiar.
He ducked his head into his magazine, afraid of being seen to covet his neighbour's wife.

The next layer peeled away as he realized this was no
neighbour, that he knew this woman from farther off
and deeper down, and he considered the possibility
that she was a friend of Annie's, in which case (the
case that it was possible) he had to arrange his face,
ready to say hello, or to stand ready to seem to look
through her if the woman did not know him.

The last layer peeled away with the realization that
she was so familiar in some other context that she was
probably somebody famous, someone on television,
Barbara Walters perhaps, and then he realized he had
known her all his life and he contemplated a jocular
assault. (Once, in Eaton's linens' department, he had
surprised his own wife bending to look at some towels
on sale, goosing her, getting the satisfying reaction
from her of a leap across the aisle and a turn in mid-air
ending in a martial crouch ten years before Tai Kwon
Do had appeared in Canada. But he'd had to explain
to the assistant who was watching that she was his
wife, and the assistant seemed to think that made
things worse.)

And then, just as he realized who she was, she
looked up like one knowing that the camera is on her
and said, 'Hello, Charlie.'

'Julie Peters. Thirty-four years.'

'I thought it was thirty-three, but never mind. How
are you?'

I should have checked her hands, he thought. Inky fingers and slightly dirty fingernails still. It was a detail on the eighteen-year-old-girl he thought she would have grown out of by now, but the unkempt nails were still there, unobscured by the remains of the day-before-yesterday's varnish she had put on before she left home. It betrayed her then and still did, the attractive girl draping the right clothes on herself because it was an occasion, but unwilling to spend enough time on a frivolous feminine image.

Whenever she had come to mind over the years he had added a bit more to his understanding. She had been fiercely intelligent, irritated by her sex, a potential bluestocking who watched the mating rites of the undergraduates with an amusement that did not quite mask her own uncertainty about how to participate, wanting to be touched, but staying out of range, wanting complete protection before she exposed herself.

They had come together as first year undergraduates, collided slightly, and then she was gone, transferring in second year to McGill. That summer she had written to him twice, but he had not replied, not feeling close enough to her to want to develop into a letter-writing old friend. Later he realized that her long, chatty, anecdotal epistles, witty, full of well-made sentences but awkward at the close, were perfect images of her desire to stay in touch but just out of range. She was keeping the lines open, but warily.

They met briefly in the fall before the second year began for coffee at Diana Sweet's, and he still liked the look of her but could not get the signals right, if she was giving off any. She was very nervous—she talked non-stop with her head swivelling continually around to see who was in the restaurant, or to avoid too much eye contact—and he was almost certain that the sexual tension was not provided by him alone. He thought she wanted to be wooed, but he suspected that her panic if he tried would take the form of artificial amusement and he wasn't risking that, so they relapsed again into a kind of teasing which kept the other still at bay.

They met again at Christmas, apparently to compare notes: Salter wasn't sure. 'How's your love-life?' she had asked, somewhere in the middle of a chat about something else. They were drinking beer in the King Cole Room and for once he had the advantage as he realized she was still unfamiliar with beer parlours, even student hangouts, and her way of looking gaily around the room was really a way of checking how she should be in the circumstances, to make sure she wasn't in a room full of drunks and whores, or if she was, to show she didn't mind. At any rate he was more at home than she was until she put the question.

When he tried to reply, she danced away again, nodding and cutting him off after three words. In fact, Salter's last girl had been a chemistry major, a small blonde girl whom he had taken home from a sock hop (this was 1958) in University College, who had lifted him into adulthood by expecting to be made love to on the couch after she had assured her parents by calling up the stairs that she was home safe. They had continued seeing each other on Saturday nights for a couple of months, but their relationship never got off the couch because they had almost nothing in common, and she was naturally taciturn, though clever at science. Then one Saturday she was busy, and he never saw her again, and he assumed that he had failed in some area that he was unaware of. Nevertheless, Wendy had conferred on him a species of manhood not all that common in 1958, and left him free to choose in future.

Now, sitting in the King Cole Room (in 1958) the young Salter wondered if he was speaking and acting differently in subtle ways as the result of having achieved a sex life, and he preened at the possibility, because he saw now that this was what had always been going on between them. She wanted to know about sex, preferably vicariously (her father was a United Church missionary) and she assumed that the Cabbagetown boy came from a culture that had them tumbling each other in the backs of cars from about the age of twelve.

'Do I know her?' she danced back into the discussion, looking around now to show it was just chat, she was not really interested.

'I doubt it. She wasn't at Vic.'

'A local girl?'

He knew what she meant. A girl from Cabbagetown. Not quite a woman of the town, but nearly. He could see she was working hard, trying for clues to track Salter's progress through the stews.

'She was from Toronto. A chemistry major.'

'A brain?' She looked for an exit. 'Was? Did she drop out?'

'It didn't last.'

'That's too bad. I'm sure someone else will be along.'

The sisterly, patronizing note was probably her effort to say something appropriate in an area which was unfamiliar territory, but it grated. 'What about you?' he had said. 'Still a virgin?'

This was not as brutal as it looks. Such licence they had granted each other in their bantering encounters in the student cafeteria.

She was equal to it. 'I'm at McGill!' she cried. 'Haven't you heard about us? Now I must go. I have to help Daddy with his sermon.'

A joke, and yet not a joke. Messages, messages, and the chief one was that she wasn't ready to reveal herself.

Salter dropped out of university after Christmas. He had found himself counting the bricks on the classroom wall during a discussion of a poem he had not read and did not intend to, and he was doing the same thing in History, Economics and Sociology. There followed a brief interlude when he tried and failed to run away to sea but lacked the necessary union card, and then, meeting a detective on a factory-league hockey team, he had joined the police.

Now, after thirty years and two marriages, he was back, picking up vibrations from Julie Peters, wondering if anything ever changes. 'I'm fine. Still a virgin?'

A young man on the other side of the rack of books looked up, astounded.

'I've forgotten my next line,' she said. 'Which way are you walking?'

They left the store and walked out to College Street. 'Why did you say that?' she asked, rattled, but still keeping it light.

'You never answered before. I thought you might now.'

'I don't remember.' She nodded across the street to the Police headquarters. 'Back to work?'

'You've been checking up on me?'

'Not really. I happened to bump into Molly. She said you'd interrogated her.'

'Who the hell is Molly? I haven't interrogated anybody by that name.'

'Molly Pride. She's the mother in that play. The one the actor who was murdered was in.'

'Why should I know her? Who is she?'

'She was with us at Vic.'

'This is getting to be Old Home Week.' Salter looked up and down the street. 'Want a drink?' He pointed to a building at the corner of College and Yonge.

She looked at her watch, shook her head, peered up and down the street as if for her limousine, and nearly shouted, 'Sure. Why not?' loudly enough to make it clear that her response, though daring, should not be seen as a sign of any kind of acquiescence, just a mock throwing of her hat over the windmill, and they crossed the street to the Hop and Grapes.

Salter treated himself to a Creemore and brought her the gin-and-tonic she asked for. She filled the glass to the top with tonic and mixed it briskly like an Alka-Seltzer.

He drank some of his beer and relaxed. What is she seeing, he asked himself. Most of the brown hair she might remember was gone; he wasn't bald, just thin and lifeless. Small red veins had broken out on his cheeks, more on the left than the right. When he depressed his chin, he corrugated the entire area, all the way into his collar. He could hear, and he could see without glasses if the print was not too small. Salter tried to angle himself to catch his reflection in the bar mirror as he lifted his glass, then jutted his chin to cut down on the wrinkles.

'You haven't changed at all,' she said. 'Not a bit. You look exactly as you used to in History 101.'

It was a decision she had made. She might have decided to go the other way and detail the changes, but this tack gave her more to say while she was still nervous.

'You have,' Salter said.

She intoned two or three lines of verse, something to do with a pretty girl turning into a hag.

'No way,' he protested, not recognizing the lines but catching the drift. 'I was thinking of propositioning you in that bookstore. Before I recognized you.'

'Pouff,' she said, blowing a lot of air through her lips to dispel this silly talk.

'You look terrific,' he said.

She grimaced as if he had flicked a few drops of beer over her. 'Tell me what you've been doing, Charlie. You've become a policeman.'

'That's it. I became one thirty-three years ago.'

'Chief Inspector, Molly said.'

'We don't have those. Staff Inspector. What about you?'

She looked at him consideringly. "Married? Of course you are.'

'Twice. Once for a year. Then for good. Two kids, boys, one at university, one still at school but wants to be an actor. How about you?'

'I'm a grandmother.'

'Who did you marry?'

'A biologist. I did science after all. I met him in graduate school.'

'A Ph.D., of course.'

She shrugged. The remark was gauche. 'Charlie Salter,' she said, making it sound like *little* Charlie Salter. 'The great detective.'

'You live in Toronto?'

'Ottawa. Bill is a dean. I don't teach any more.'

'What are you doing here?'

'I came for a meeting. I work for a relief organization.'

He knew without asking that she was chairperson of whatever it was. Everything about her proclaimed that she expected to be looked at a lot. 'How long are you here for?'

'Two weeks. I arrived on Saturday.'

Why would she tell him that? 'We should get together.'

'I'd like to meet your wife.'

'You can't. She's in Prince Edward Island, looking after her father.'

'Maybe next time, then. Quite a shock, bumping into you like that. Now I must run.'

'We could have dinner. Where are you staying?'

'The Chelsea Inn. No. I have to meet some colleagues. We're eating at the hotel.'

'I'll walk you over. It's just a couple of blocks.'

Now she looked flustered. 'No, no. I have to run.' She gathered up her book and purse. 'You have another drink.' She patted his hand.

'I'll call you.'

'We have a very tight schedule. All right, if you want. We can probably find half an hour for a chat.'

BACK AT HEADQUARTERS, the cadet on duty at the inquiry desk told him that a mature-type lady had been looking for him, didn't leave her name, dressed in red. 'I told her I'd seen you go into the College Park building.'

Not quite a coincidence, then.

SEVEN

THE DEPUTY CHIEF was still in his office. 'Seen Horvarth yet?' he asked, as soon as Salter walked in.

'Tomorrow,' Salter said.

'I'd like to get this thing settled.' He passed a finger below his lip, scratched a rough spot on the corner of his mouth, then picked lightly at the inside edge of his nostril, finishing by kneading the top of his nose with two fingers and a thumb. 'What's happening with that dead actor?' he said finally.

Salter recounted what he had learned so far. 'It still looks like a mob thing.'

The deputy grunted. 'Now you know as much as the rest of us. Start digging, will you? I'd like to see the end of that, too.'

'I'M GOING TO TALK to one of the actresses in the play,' Salter told Peterman.

Peterman stood up and began to put on his jacket.

'You don't have to come along. Later on we may have to talk to everyone he knew.'

'What's so special about this one?'

'I want to get an idea of what the other people in the play felt about him.'

'So why her?'

'I think she might be the best place to start digging.'

'Why?'

'Someone told me I knew her in college.'

Peterman took off his jacket and sat down. 'That right? The advantage of an education, I guess.'

FIRST HE DROVE out to see Horvarth. He considered the tactic of seeming to need Horvarth's expertise on the Hunter case, then abandoned it in favour of a direct approach.

The sergeant lived on Glencairn Avenue in a pleasant sixty-year-old house with a huge back yard. The original plot had apparently been laid out when land in this part of Toronto was still cheap. Since then the subway had arrived nearby, and Toronto had boomed so that houses in this part of town had increased in value to the point where no young police sergeant could hope to afford one. The mortgage would equal his salary.

Horvarth showed Salter through the house and into the yard, where he had been mowing the lawn. He watched Salter appraise the house, then said, 'It belonged to my wife's parents. Her father was a schoolteacher and he bought this in nineteen fifty-nine for twenty thousand. They say it's now worth six hundred thousand.'

A familiar story. 'Do they live with you?' Salter asked.

Horvarth shook his head. 'He died. Shirley's mother refuses to live with us—Shirley's the only daughter—and the deal is we pay the rent on her apartment and we get the house sooner rather than later. It's a break for us. Shirley was born here.'

Salter said, 'The deputy sent me out to ask you to come in for a chat.'

Horvarth wound the cord around the handle of the mower and brushed his hand clean against his pants. 'Want some coffee?'

'Sure.' Salter sat down on one of the chairs set out around the table on Horvarth's deck. 'Just cream.'

When he returned with the coffee, Horvarth said, 'He could have called. I'm here.'

'You might not have gone, though. I mean, you would have gone, but you might not have told him anything.'

'That's possible.' Horvarth leaned over to put his coffee cup on the deck, and settled himself in his chair.

'What are you up to, Joe?'

'You asking for the deputy?' Horvarth took off one of his mocassins and banged it against the deck to get rid of grass clippings.

'He isn't after your neck. Yet.'

'Yes, he is. He has to be.'

'He has a problem. He's got pictures of you taking money.'

'Pictures? Who took them?'

'I don't know.'

'Nor do I. He does, though. I'd like to find out.' Horvarth went to work to clean off his other shoe.

'That it? You want to know who is behind it?'

'Yeah.'

'From the pictures I saw, it doesn't make much difference.'

'It does to me. If they bring me before a formal tribunal, then I'll find out, won't I?'

'If they do that, you could lose your job. Depending on what rules they play by, you could go to jail. How's that prospect?'

Horvarth gave a nod to indicate that he had considered the prospect. 'What does he want?'

'He's from the old school. What's that phrase that politicians use?—damage control. He wants to control the damage. But he doesn't want to be accused of a cover-up, not with this new police commission. He's retiring soon, and he doesn't want any messy police corruption stuff just before he goes. On the other hand, if he has to, if he thinks it could get messy for him, he'll let it happen.'

'So he wants a little chat in his office, just me and him, to find out how he can manage me with the least damage?'

'That's it.'

'No.'

'No, what?'

'I'll tell you this much. Sir. If we have a little chat, that would be the end of it. He'd be satisfied, and I'd be rehabilitated. But *I* wouldn't be satisfied. I want an inquiry.'

'Christ, I've seen the pictures, Joe. You got an answer to them?'

'I told you, I'm reserving my defence. Get you some more coffee?'

Salter held out his cup. He needed a new opening.

When Horvarth returned with the coffee, Salter said, 'All right. I'll tell Mackenzie. I think I know what will happen. He'll say, the hell with it, and proceed with an inquiry. But if you're being cute, he'll throw you to the wolves. If you don't have an answer to those pictures, and I don't see how you can have, and you come up in public with some kind of bullshit defence that damages his division, he'll hold on to your legs while they hang you. On the other hand, if it isn't you in those pictures but your twin brother or some such, it will still make the papers and he's still going to be unhappy. So I don't see what you're going to gain.'

Horvarth shrugged in reflex, and Salter changed the subject to give the message time to sink in. 'I met Taber, the bookie, yesterday, and he told me what I wanted to know. But that only applies to him and the people he knows. I need to know if *anybody* took bets from Hunter.'

'Did Taber actually *meet* you?'

'In the Mercury Hotel.'

'Jesus.' Horvarth smiled slightly. 'He wanted to get a message across.'

'The message he gave me was that you're not on the take.'

'Can't trust a bookie, though, can you? What else?'

'That Hunter was not known to him.'

'Ask him again. He's got very good contacts. He'll be able to find out if Hunter's been known to bet with anybody.'

'You ask him. Give him a call. Tell him that it's important to you. Tell him I need to know, and it might do you some good. Because whatever the hell you're playing at now, the day might come when you'll be glad someone has a good word to say for you.'

Horvarth looked at him in surprise. 'All right. But I'll have him call you.'

'Who's the guy in the pictures, Joe?'

'How do I know? I haven't seen them.' Horvarth looked out at the garden.

I'll ask his pals on the squad, Salter thought. I'll ask Taber. He put his cup down and stood up. 'Well, I tried,' he said.

As he was leaving, Horvarth asked, 'Who would be involved in this little chat that Mackenzie wants?'

'Just him and you.'

Horvarth shook his head. 'Not enough. I want to see the whites of their eyes. And I want to know whether it's one thing or several. I need an inquiry.'

He walked Salter to his car, and Salter waited for him to add something, but he just waved and walked back to the house. Salter left him setting up his electric mower.

MOLLY PRIDE WAS A FRUMP, a middle-aged actress without warpaint who looked like Salter's mental image of a washerwoman. Her hair was flattened under a kind of string skullcap, her face was ashy and dry-skinned and her teeth were yellow from chain-smoking. Salter talked to her in the theatre, two hours before her performance.

'You didn't know Hunter before this play, I was told,' Salter began.

'That's right. And he never took any interest in me here, either.' She spoke with a hint of irony, perfectly aware of her lack of attraction to someone like Hunter.

'Did he have any—friends—among the women here?'

'Not that I know of. He was running out of surprises, widely known to be a shit of the first water.'

'None of the male actors liked him, I gather.'

'The nearest thing he had to a friend was Turgeon, the stage manager. Why are you asking me? I had no interest in the bastard.'

Salter looked at his watch. 'You're an onlooker. Sometimes they see more.'

'Oh yeah?' She smiled comfortably. Salter wondered if she knew what he was up to, and if an opening would occur for him to introduce his real interest.

'Don't you have to get ready?' There were sounds now from the area beyond the stage. Behind them, high under the roof, someone was moving about among the lights. As Salter looked up, a spotlight lit up the stage and went out.

'Russell,' she said. 'The lighting man.'

'He sit up there all through the play?'

'He practically lives up there.'

Once more the spotlight came up, then died as all the houselights came on. Salter turned back to Molly Pride. 'A good play?' he asked.

'Perry can write. Usually I play salt-of-the-earth women, but he's given me a real part. But to make it work I have to give them something to play against. Stay and watch and you'll see it. All through the first act I have to leave room for the character that comes out in the second. Brilliant, I am.' She smiled broadly, mocking herself. Then she added, 'It's true, though. It's the part I've been waiting for. I know the woman

I'm playing. She's the sacrificer. All through the first act you find out how much of her family she's sacrificed to keep things her way. She's given up her life for them, is how she sees it, and she doesn't like it when they try to have lives of their own, apart from her. Come and see it again and watch how I turn from nurturer to devourer.'

'Julie Peters thought you were sensational.' That should do it.

'She found you, did she? I'm glad she liked it. She said you were at Vic. I don't remember you.'

'I didn't stay long.'

'Long enough to meet our Julie, though. Did you date her, whatever that meant back then? Not much if I knew Julie.' She lit a fresh cigarette from the butt of the old one.

'Not so's you'd notice. How did my name crop up?'

'She came backstage afterwards. Tell you the truth, I hardly remembered her, so I was kind of surprised the way she came on to me. Then I remembered. She headed up the Student Christian Movement, and was first year president and all that shit. I wasn't into any of that. Yeah. She asked me what you looked like now, but I hadn't met you. How did she know you were doing the investigation?'

'You must have dropped the name.'

'Me? It didn't ring any bells with me until she started talking about you. Even then, frankly, I couldn't remember you.' She leaned back and looked at him through a cloud of smoke, then shook her head. 'I still can't. How did she find you?'

'We bumped into each other in a bookshop.'

'Well, well. If I had a better memory we could have a reunion. Now I have to go. Sorry I couldn't be more help with Hunter.'

'I got what I came for.'

'There's Bill now. Bill, come and meet the nice policeman. Tell him about Hunter.'

Salter had seen him hovering nearby, repairing a hinge on a scenery door. He was a small square man, heavily built, with wire-rimmed glasses and a large handlebar moustache. He put down his screwdriver and came towards them, wiping his hands on his pants.

Salter stood up. 'Metro police,' he said. 'Miss Pride says I should talk to you. You knew Hunter better than anyone, I hear.'

'Miss who?' He looked in the direction of the disappearing Molly. 'Oh, Molly. sorry. Didn't recognize the name.' Turgeon laughed.

Salter recognized the facetiousness as a need to get comfortable in his presence.

Molly Pride shouted from the wings. 'In future that's how I want to be addressed by common stagehands.'

Turgeon found a chair for himself, and the two men sat down. 'What can I do for you, sir?' Turgeon crossed his arms and put a helping look on his face.

'Tell me about Hunter. You were his closest pal.'

'You make it sound like we were bum buddies,' Turgeon laughed. 'You obviously haven't heard about Alec.'

'So tell me.'

'Well, in the first place, apart from acting, all he cared about was women. He was a sexaholic. Is that a word? Sounds like a maniac, but I think he was just plain greedy. It's a funny thing, though, they all knew about him, everybody in the business knew it, but he still had no trouble landing them. Afterwards they might hate him, but first they said yes.'

'I've talked to Connie Spurling. She seemed to think that all that had finished once she and Hunter got together.'

'She believes that, does she?' Turgeon looked knowing. 'Fact is, all she did was make it a bit spicier for him. He liked living on the edge. She was someone you wouldn't want as an enemy and yet he got as big a kick out of fooling her as he did out of doing it.'

'How long did you know him?'

'Not all that long. I met him last summer at Brighton when I was working there.'

'Did you like the guy?'

Turgeon considered the question. 'You'll find out there wasn't much to like in the ordinary sense. Women were attracted to him for the usual reasons. But men weren't. He didn't care. Fucking and acting was all he cared about. And gambling. I've forgotten the question. Right, did I like him? Let's say he didn't bother me the way he did some. I got along with him all right.'

'What did you have in common?'

'Nothing. I did some favours for him.'

'Like what.'

'Mostly I provided alibis.'

'Why?'

'Because he asked me to. Because of Connie Spurling. I decided anything I could do to upset her would be in a good cause, so I told her stories about Alec, covered up his escapades. You have to know that woman. She made life a goddamn misery, in Brighton and here. I couldn't stand the cow. She treated me like something you would scrape off your shoe.'

'You covered for him regularly?'

'Whenever called on.'

'What did you know about his gambling?'

Turgeon shook his head. 'I know it killed him.'

'Was he gambling in Brighton?'

'I'm sure he was, but I didn't have anything to do with that side of him. It's a pastime for morons, I told him.'

'Who did he bet with?'

'I think he went to the track at Fort Erie.'

'No bookies?'

'He never mentioned any to me. If he did, I would think he'd have to go to Niagara Falls. There weren't any bookies in Brighton. As I say, I never knew much about that side of him except that lately it got a lot worse. I'm pretty sure there were people looking for him. A couple of times he asked me to check the lobby of his apartment building before he would get out of the car when I gave him a ride home after the show. I never actually saw anyone but what else could he be afraid of?'

'Did you see him or talk to him the day he was killed?'

'That was a Sunday, wasn't it? No. We didn't socialize. He left the theatre Saturday night and that was the last I saw of him. She picked him up.'

There were voices coming from the back of the auditorium. Turgeon looked at his watch.

'Have you seen her since?' Salter asked.

'I went to her office to see if there was anything I could do and she told me to get lost. She was suffering, of course. No doubt about that. Now I have to get this show started.'

Salter stood up. Molly Pride reappeared in the wings. 'Say hello to Julie for me,' she called. 'Tell her thanks for the compliments.'

HE LEFT THE THEATRE, found a call-box, and called the Chelsea Inn. At six-thirty she might still be in her room. 'I'm free for dinner tonight, too,' he began, without saying hello.

'I have to work, I'm afraid,' she said immediately.

'Some kind of meeting? What time?'

'No, no. I have to get caught up with the paperwork. We've had endless meetings and now I'm swamped. Where are you?'

'I'm at the Estragon Theatre, talking to Molly Pride.'

'What about?'

'I'm investigating a murder, remember.'

'What did Molly have to say?'

'She was very helpful.'

'Was she? Good. Now I have to get back to work.'

'Don't you have to eat?'

'I was just going to have something here. Did Molly remember you?'

'No. Where does "here" mean?'

'Hereabouts.'

'Meet me in the lobby at seven.'

'I just want a sandwich.'

'You'll be a cheap date.'

HE TOOK HER AT HER WORD and they walked along Yonge Street to where he had eaten the night before, the Pickle Barrel, a restaurant whose menu is designed for officeworkers during the day and families of tourists at night, and where no one seeing them through the glass walls could accuse them of having a secret rendezvous. Just two old friends celebrating a serendipitous encounter.

His beer and her glass of wine arrived, and she said, 'Well, how are you?' and looked around the room to show him and anyone else watching what fun it was to bump into each other like this. 'What did Molly have to say? Oh no, I asked that. Tell me about your family.'

'I already did. Tell me about yours.'

'Three daughters,' she said, holding up the same number of fingers. 'One grandson.'

'But you don't work. Just this volunteer stuff.'

'Just an old-fashioned wife of an old-fashioned dean.' Expressions chased each other across her face as she sought to get comfortable.

'Got a picture of him?'

'Not on me.'

'In your room?'

When she did not respond he knew that the word alarmed her.

'What happened to your first marriage?' she countered.

'We were incompatible.'

'Totally.'

'Not totally. Just in every other way.'

She blushed slightly. It had always been part of the game that she would refuse to be offended, because, as the missionary's daughter but wanting to be treated as a normal person, she was not certain what was decorous. Then she said, 'Wasn't that enough?' and laughed and picked up the menu to show that she was indifferent to the answer. They had not progressed an inch in thirty years.

'At first it was, then it wasn't.'

'Did I know her? Was she your little girl in Chemistry?'

'No. I married a Fine Arts student. Then I married my wife, who is from Prince Edward Island and works in advertising but is presently on the Island looking after her father.'

'And here you are, faithfully keeping the home fires burning.'

'That's right.' He sipped his beer. 'Come on, let's have it. Your life history. The works. You first, then I'll tell you mine.'

'All right,' she said. 'Stop me when you're bored.'

As she talked, he understood that nothing had changed; not her, certainly; not them. The wrinkles, an eye that looked permanently slightly bloodshot, the encroaching grey in her hair, were all irrelevant. What mattered was what had stayed the same: her self-consciousness, her uncertainty about how to behave so as not to compromise herself and yet to make it clear that she was choosing not to compromise herself and might choose differently tomorrow. She never had, though. They had been sexually attracted from the beginning, but in the late 'fifties at Victoria College, sexual attraction was no impediment to virginity. Innocence was rampant—a girl called Pussy was running for student office—and there was always more talk than action.

What really kept them apart was the class system. Salter was working class, Julie from the Methodist middle; each found the other exotic to a degree that made it difficult to close the gap. The result of their attraction was a kind of endlessly charged conversation that never developed into a concrete proposition. It would be hard to imagine now, Salter thought. The distance between the 'fifties and the 'eighties was far greater than the distance between Salter's generation and the Victorians. His own son at university could not know what difficulties his parents had laboured under, finding, apparently, none himself. And yet he and Julie had achieved a kind of intimacy, different from the kind he shared with Annie, an intimacy which had survived because the element of curiosity still fuelled it, a spark which consummation would have quenched. But it was the reason why all wives resent the old college girlfriends. Something had been shared that the wife could never have.

She finished and made a gesture indicating it was his turn. He delivered the bones of his life, and stopped. 'You're not listening,' he said.

'I'm looking. You haven't changed at all.'

'You said that.' He looked up at the clock. 'Let's go for a walk.'

She looked at her watch and affected surprise, shaking her head. 'Walk me back to the hotel.'

In the lobby of the hotel, she said, 'There's some of my committee in the coffee shop,' and waved to them through the glass. 'I'll see you.' She turned to the elevators.

'It's OK for you to kiss me. Everybody does it now, and I don't think we ever did.'

'Oh, stop it. Of course we did.' But she let him, and thirty years rolled away because she still wasn't sure how to avoid giving the wrong signals, or the right ones. Before she could move away, he gave her a hug, not done in 1958, and still, for him, and probably for her, rare and heavily freighted.

'What's your room number?' he asked, releasing her and wishing to leave open the possibility, or not, that he was joking.

'Stop it, I told you,' and she fled into the elevator.

THERE WAS NO SIGN of Seth at home, and no message. He called Annie, feeling mildly unfaithful.

'You sound cheerful,' she said.

'Carefree,' he corrected. 'I don't give a curse. It's spring here. What's it like there?'

'Raining, of course. What do you mean? Have you caught the person who killed that actor?'

'No, and we won't, either, and I don't give a curse. I said that, didn't I? It's spring.'

'Have you been drinking?'

"Soda water. It's the effervescence. How's it going?'

'I'll call you tomorrow.'

He understood. Mother was in the room.

'How's Seth's play coming? When are you going to see it?'

'Is he expecting me to?'

'Of course he is. Dear God. Have a little chat with him, would you? This isn't the end-of-the-term play. It's his life.'

'I'll wait up for him. Call me.'

WHEN SETH CAME HOME, Salter made all the right noises and fixed a time when he could see the play. Having mended his fences, he then smashed them down. 'I'm investigating the homicide of an actor,' he said.

'I know, Dad. Alec Hunter. He was in *After Paris*.'

'Good play. You should go see it.'

Seth barely stopped on his way upstairs. 'I have seen it. I went with Grandfather two months ago. You were busy, as I remember.'

EIGHT

THE WEATHER the next morning remained splendid and Salter found himself still not very much involved in Hunter's death. An actor had made the mistake of getting in debt to the mob, that was all there was to it. At some time, in ten years perhaps, some mobster would tell them who did it in exchange for a few years off his sentence. Thus Salter wanted to believe so he could hand it back to Homicide for all of the hard work necessary to explore all the other possibilities. If it weren't for Hunter, he could go fishing. Details nagged, the chief one being that a thousand dollars, as Taber the bookie had said, was not the kind of sum the mob usually killed for. But there would be another reason, no doubt. In the meantime, he would do what could be done.

At the office he was met by the reporter who had caused all the trouble by first inflaming the Italian community, then by arousing the suspicions of the non-Italian community. There was time and room to dodge him, but Salter decided to see what the man wanted.

To know if there were any developments, of course, and what they were, and if not, what the police had been doing.

We have a number of leads, Salter thought. Then he thought of another answer, one more in tune with his mood, and also one that might produce a reaction that could be lively, like throwing a lighted match into a box of fireworks. Energized by his insight, he took a slightly hostile tone to the reporter. 'None at all,' he said. 'And I don't think we will, either, until the community, especially the Italian community, realizes they are shielding a gang of vicious killers. Somewhere out there someone knows who this killer is, or knows someone who knows. But no one is coming forward. There isn't a lot we can do if the citizens won't cooperate.'

The reporter, Huey, scribbled hard. 'You think it was the work of organized crime?'

'I think it was the Mafia.'

'What makes you sure?'

'I said I *think*. I'm not sure, just guessing, for the same reasons you put in your first story. The method is one they use, the garrotte or ligature, the room was booked by someone with an Italian accent, and there was a gambling debt involved.'

'The community, that is, the Italian community, objected to being smeared by this. They said it was just a room clerk jumping to conclusions, that there's no reason to suppose the killer was Italian.'

The only colour or suspected race you can mention these days is Vietnamese, Salter thought, because they aren't organized like the rest of us. And then there was a gender bias. Any day now Salter expected to see a headline, 'Two Gunpersons Kill Storekeeper'.

'I think there are reasons,' he said. 'I think it was a Mafia killing. Our information is that the Mafia is mostly Italian.' Huey looked up sharply. 'So I'm looking for a male, five-feet eleven to six feet, with a gold tooth and an Italian accent. Oh yes, and I am seeking the cooperation of the Italian community, the vast majority of whom are law-abiding.'

Huey scribbled his way off the page, and looked up. 'Do you realize how many city councillors, MPPs and MPs are of Italian origin, Staff Inspector?'

'I should think nearly as many as there are cops. Now go away and write a story about how biased I am.'

Huey left looking excited and thoughtful.

Next, Salter considered calling Julie for breakfast and actually dialled the hotel number before hanging up. He called Annie instead.

'Something's wrong,' she said immediately.

'I just thought I'd see how things were going.'

'Since last night? Let's see, we went to bed, then we got up. I can't think of anything else. What's the matter?'

'Nothing. I miss you. Are the lilacs still out there?'

'What brought this on?'

'I don't know. Spring. You remember the hotel we stayed at in England? The one with the dog?'

'The Plough. In Clanfield. Why?'

'I was just remembering it, too.'

'I'll be back as soon as I can.'

'When did we cut down the lilacs?'

'I'll bring you some back. They're still in bloom here. Now I have to go. Call me when you've seen Seth's play.'

Salter hung up and considered the options. As Peterman walked in to his office, he decided what they had to do. 'We're going to a play,' he said.

'You and your wife? I thought she was away.'

'No. Us. You and me.'

'A play? Us? When?'

'Tonight.'

'What kind of play?'

'The one Hunter was in. I've talked to Hunter's only friend in the company, and to one of the actresses. Now we'd better talk to the rest of them.'

'We have to go, eh? Both of us.'

'Don't you usually work in pairs?'

'With suspects, yes. Not if we're just ...'

'Farting around? It'll give us a good look at them, and someone may know something about his private life.'

'He was a gambler who got in over his head. Maybe I could meet you afterwards?'

'You have something else important on?'

'Yes and no.'

Salter felt the need to let Peterman know who was in charge. 'I'll pick you up here. Seven-thirty.'

'I'll call my wife.'

Now, having the rest of the day, he turned to the 'position paper'. Then, justifying himself by the thought that he would be working that night, he pushed the paper aside, left the office, played a game of squash, then went home to cut the grass in case Annie suddenly came back.

'IT'S NOT EVEN a proper theatre,' Peterman said, as they approached the door. 'It's a *shed*. We'll probably have to sit on the fucking floor. Let's hope to Christ they have lines, not some improvisation.'

The play was called *After Paris*. The first act was set in White Plains, Saskatchewan: the living-room of the Palmer farmhouse. The second was set in the same place, the next day.

'It's a Canadian play.' Peterman looked stricken. 'On a farm. In Saskatchewan. It'll be about the Depression. There'll be an old fart trickling soil through his fingers talking about how many stumps he's cleared with these hands. There'll be a guy from the bank in a black hat. And Ma. She'll tell us about how she buried her first born right in that field where that rose-bush is growing. And there'll be three kids saying, "Don't give up, Pa," over and over. And there'll be an old dog that dies. And someone playing mouth organ backstage.'

'You've seen it?'

'It used to be on CBC a lot. About twenty years ago, before we all got cable. Maybe they're still doing it.'

'This play?'

'The one I described. I doubt if it's changed much.'

'This one is set in the present.'

Peterman brightened. 'Not the Depression?' He thought for a moment. 'Incest, then. It'll be about incest.'

'Where did I get the impression you don't go to plays?'

'Not since nineteen seventy. But I read the *Star*. All Canadian plays are about incest now.'

They bought their tickets so as not to excite too much interest backstage before they were ready, and passed through a curtain into what had one time been a pickle warehouse, now the Estragon Theatre. There were no individual seats: a bench ran round the walls, and several rows of similar benches had been bolted to a steeply raked floor. The whole arrangement was reminiscent of a small touring circus tent. The stage, or playing space, was at one end of the room, but not separated from it. Salter and Peterman sat at the back on one of the raised benches which was too far from the wall and too close to the ground for Salter's comfort, but it seemed to fit Peterman's thick body and short legs perfectly.

The lights went down and an old man in suspenders came on in front of the set, bent down and made motions of testing the earth. Peterman looked evenly at Salter.

'No mouth organ yet,' Salter pointed out.

'Be a train whistle first.'

'Do you mind!' a girl sitting in front of them demanded.

But Peterman turned out to be agreeably misinformed. The play's title referred to the popular song and underscored the theme which dealt with the difficult return visit of a Torontonian to his family home. The occasion was a wedding, the marriage of the returning hero's sister to an old boyhood chum of the hero's. The first act concerned the sentimental laying out of the hero's memories of the others in a series of funny and wistful scenes, memories of time spent with his sister, his brother, his sister-in-law (an old girlfriend passed on to his brother) and his parents, as well as an aged grandmother. An odd undercurrent ran through the dialogue, and Salter realized that a delicate element of parody was present, a note of mockery that undercut the sentiment and suggested that the memories, the values, and even the kind of play apparently embodying them were all being framed for inspection. The act ended as they all left for the church, and now the accompanying music, 'Bringing in the Sheaves' played on a tinny organ, dared the audience to take it solemnly.

The second act was a reprise of the first: the memories were the same but this time, after a certain amount of drink, the others did the remembering. What the hero remembered as a petting scene in the first act was now seen through the girl's eyes as rape. Old grudges were brought up, scores were settled, and the audience was left with a transformed understanding of the hero's relationship to his family. One of the discoveries, which the hero was helped to by his brother, was that his mother, in Act One a legendary figure of Junoesque dimensions who held the family together, was just as capable of being seen as the villain who had denied all of them their room to grow. Thus Act Two re-examined the values of Act One and revealed, as all the clichés were stood on their heads, that Act One was to be read as a critical commentary on just the kind of play that Peterman had feared. The play ended when the father left, determined, now his responsibilities to his family were over, to spend his last years irresponsibly. It was a weak ending, as if the playwright having found a truth did not know what it would do to these people, but in the main Salter found the play funny, moving and totally absorbing.

When the hero appeared onstage at the beginning of Act One, holding a suitcase and saying, 'Anybody home?' Peterman closed his eyes and slept through to the intermission. 'I get embarrassed,' he said. 'All those people supposed to be in a living-room shouting at you from twenty feet away. It's like they're...'

'Acting?'

'Yeah.'

He stayed awake for ten uncomfortable minutes in the second act until the hero, alone on stage, began a soliloquy, then turned away and closed his eyes.

NINE

As the play drew to a conclusion, Salter slipped out to the foyer, where he found Turgeon, the stage manager, and gave him the message that he and Peterman wanted to talk to everyone for a few minutes afterwards.

They conducted the interviews on stage.

Salter grouped two armchairs and a rocking-chair around a coffee table; Peterman took the rocking-chair, rested his feet on the lower rung, rocked himself back and forth several times in a testing fashion, then took out his notebook. Salter asked the cast to wait in the back of the theatre for him to call them. They began with the hero.

'Could I get your name, sir?' Peterman asked.

'It's in the programme. Keith Walker.'

Still in his make-up, Walker was tall and good-looking. His blond hair was carefully and stylishly cut to fit his rôle, that of a bond trader at the peak of his powers.

'Nice play, Keith,' Peterman said. 'You were very good.'

'Thank you.'

'What part did Hunter have?'

'Mine.'

'We were lucky, then. In a sense, that is. To get you, I mean. Kind of a silver lining.'

'You understudied him, did you?' Salter asked.

'I prepared for the rôle, yes, once we realized that the play would continue after his contract ran out. When he was playing it I played the brother.'

'So the brother we saw, he's new to the part?'

'He did the same thing. He played the sister's husband before, and prepared for the part I was playing.'

Peterman looked at his programme. 'So who's playing Matera's old part?'

'Perry, Perry Adler. The writer/director. He's playing it himself.'

Peterman rocked himself forward, swinging his feet on to the floor. 'I should get this laid out.' He put his notebook on his knee and took the programme in his left hand. He divided the notebook into three columns and headed them 'Actor's name', 'was', and 'is'. 'Now. You—what's the name again—Keith Walker, right—you were the brother, now you're the hero. Matera was the brother-in-law, now is the brother, and Adler was the guy who wrote the play, now is the brother-in-law. The women: they all still the same?'

'Yes.'

'And Dad is still Manny Perlmutter?'

'Yes.'

'And Bill Turgeon is the stage manager.'

'Yes. Yes.'

'Who else?'

'Nobody else.'

'What about all the helpers?'

'If you mean the crew, a student from Ryerson does the lights; there's a make-up girl; and all the rest— ticketsellers, ushers and so on—are also students.'

'Are they all waiting back there now?' Salter asked.

Walker made a one-armed expansive gesture towards the end of the auditorium.

'We won't need them all at this point. Ask the students to come forward and give their names, and they can go.'

Walker stood up and boomed the message into the darkness. Three young girls came forward, and Peterman took their names while Salter chatted to Walker.

'Awkward having the star leave you after three months,' he said.

'Not in the least. Frankly, it's a much better show because it's a happier company. Much more of an ensemble.'

'You did well to step into a big part like that.' Salter was taking his lead from Peterman. Flattery was what made these people relax, lots of it.

'It was hard preparing two rôles at the same time, and trying not to let yourself be affected by the way he played it, and it's still a bit rough round the edges, because we have to carry John and Perry a bit, as Perry would be the first to tell you.'

'I thought it was wonderful. Your part, especially.'

Peterman looked up from his notebook. 'Terrific,' he said.

'It's all in the text. You just have to dig it out. Of course Alec cast a large shadow, but I'm finding places he hadn't quite got to. He had some lovely grace notes I haven't reached yet, though, so I've had to rework some of the rhythms, especially in the first act.'

'You must have worked like a sonofabitch,' Peterman said.

'That's theatre.'

'Doesn't anyone object?' Salter asked.

'We all felt the challenge, I think. Essentially we were doing a new play with hardly any rehearsal time. Anyway, there isn't a lot of other work about. There never is. And it's nice to step into a proven success. There's talk of adapting it for television.'

'TV?' Peterman was impressed. 'That'd be great. Good luck. You deserve it. I thought you were terrific.'

'Thank you. Did you find any draggy places?'

'Not when you were on stage, Keith. But the part that really got to me was the opening scene in the second act. That big speech of yours when you were alone on stage. Terrific.' Peterman shook his head in wonder.

Salter said, quickly, 'Did you know Hunter well?'

'Fairly well. I don't recall that we ever played together before, but he knew my work.'

'What kind of guy was he?' Peterman asked. 'Did you like him?'

'He's only been dead for a few days.' Walker looked as if he wanted to draw up his skirts.

'Fact is, we need to know more.'

'I suppose you do. We weren't friends, no.'

'You a better actor than him?'

Walker looked offendedly across at Salter, who smiled and said nothing. 'What on earth do you want to know that for? As a matter of fact, to save you coming back, I do—did—think I am a better actor.'

'Now you're getting a chance to prove it,' Peterman said.

'Sergeant Peterman is trying to save us time,' Salter explained. 'Hunter died in a way to suggest there may have been some shady corners in his life. That's really what we want to know about.'

'I didn't like him but we weren't enemies.' He gestured to the darkness at the back. 'They'll all tell you that.'

'Where were you when he was killed?' Peterman asked.

'What!'

Peterman looked at Salter.

'Where were you when he was killed?' Salter repeated. 'It's a routine question. You must have asked it yourself. In a murder play.'

'I was watching television.' He turned to face Peterman. '*All Creatures Great and Small*, *Mystery*, then bed. Do you want to know what happened in each episode?'

'That's OK. I watch Channel 17 Sunday nights. Were you on your own?'

'Yes, I was.'

'You married or something?' Peterman winked.

'I'm recently separated. I live alone at present.'

Salter cut in. 'Tell us about Hunter. You're the first we've talked to. What kind of person was he?'

'I know the two things everyone knew: he couldn't keep his hands off the women, and he was into gambling. That's why he got killed, didn't he?'

'We don't know why he was killed. So he was a womanchaser.'

'Ask any of the women. Ask the ushers. Excuse me a moment.' He put his thumbs under the base of his skull and peeled off the beautiful wig, showing a nearly bald head with patches of black stubble.

'Jesus,' Peterman said. 'What's your next trick?'

'It gets hot and itchy.' Walker rubbed his skull in relief. Even though his head had been scraped to the skin, the bald spots that made the wig desirable, on stage anyway, were clearly visible. 'When I let it grow, there isn't enough to need a comb...'

'Do you know any of Hunter's enemies?' Salter asked.

'Everybody he's ever worked with. Nobody in particular.'

'Did you know his girlfriend?'

'We all did. She attended every performance and took him home on a chain afterwards.'

They waited for amplification.

'She was the stage mother, the jealous wife, and someone looking after her investment, all rolled into one. She was demented about him, and I understand she bankrolled their life together. She wouldn't let another woman near him.'

'You didn't like her,' Peterman said.

'No.'

Again they waited for the more that was obviously there.

'She was the publicity person for the play. She offered to do it for nothing, and we didn't have a budget for publicity anyway, beyond a couple of tiny ads and some posters. She was good, too. Hardly a day went by without some mention of Alec in the press, or on television. Nobody else, though.'

Out of the corner of his eye, Salter could see that Peterman was losing interest, was, in fact, on the verge of falling asleep again. 'OK, thank you, Mr Walker. Where can we find you if we need you again?'

Walker gave his address and phone number to Peterman and stood up. 'Who shall I send over?' he asked.

'The writer. Mr Adler.'

'I suppose you don't want me to talk to the others.'

'What about?' Peterman wondered.

'What you've just been asking me.'

'Oh, right, yes. Well, that goes without saying, doesn't it?'

When Walker was gone, Peterman said, 'I think that proves his alibi. They're always saying stuff like that on Channel 17.'

Salter laughed. 'I was thinking, that alibi doesn't work any more, does it, not with videotape. Leave him on the list until we come up with someone better.'

Perry Adler, the writer/director, at fifty or fifty-five, was a few years too old for his rôle and awkward on stage, but since he had only seven or eight lines he did not drag the play down. He walked through the part, posturing a little when he spoke, but otherwise not interfering with the action. He had little to add to Walker's account.

'I know nothing about Hunter except as an actor,' he said.

'We hear he was good.'

'Yes, he was. He helped a lot at the beginning, but by the time he left we could manage without him. He was a better actor than Walker, I have to admit—' he looked over his shoulder quickly—'but the play is strong enough to carry the actor.'

'How much longer will it run?'

'Another three weeks. Then we go to Chicago. We've been picked up by the Apollo theatre there.'

'That good?'

'I'm very happy with it.'

'Would you rather have gone with Hunter?'

'His contract had expired, and I was glad of it. He had a lot of baggage.'

'Baggage?'

'His agent. His ego.'

'Hunter's movie folded, did you know? He was available after all.'

'And I believe Connie Spurling let the Chicago management know. And I believe they wanted him. So we were coming to a crunch. But we didn't need him.'

'Will you take the rest of the cast?'

'Walker, Matera, and Penny Wicklow. The rest aren't free.'

Peterman asked, 'Penny Wicklow?' He looked at the programme and wrote in his notebook. 'She Granny?'

'That's her.'

'Now the Chicago people knew Hunter was free, might they have insisted on Hunter?' Salter asked.

'When they saw the play first, he was in it, and they weren't sure but that he was key. But I got them to come up to look at the new cast before Hunter was free and they were satisfied enough to sign contracts. When they heard he was free they wanted to make a change, but I had a deal and I wanted them to stick to it. In fact, I was just about ready to tell them that if they wanted Hunter, they couldn't have the play, which would have been pretty ballsy of me, because it's the first time I've had this kind of offer.'

'He was that bad to work with, was he?'

'There was more to it than that. Spurling and Hunter were starting to act as if the play was some kind of rough draft for them to improve on. I'm pretty sure she paid someone to look at his part to see where it could be expanded. They were sure as hell full of suggestions, some of which I accepted in the beginning, but I've got rid of now. That's the playwright speaking. Then, from the beginning she was wondering if it was quite wise for me to direct my own play. In other words, if she'd got Hunter back in the play she'd have been on the next plane to Chicago, ready to explain to them how the play needed rewriting and Hunter needed a new director to explore his full potential.'

'You don't know this, do you?'

'Call it paranoia. But I'm not alone in that department. She's totally unscrupulous.'

'But so far, you had what you wanted. No Hunter.'

'That's right. A definition of a happy cast.'

JOHN MATERA was the newest member of the cast. He sat down without looking at them, seeming unimpressed by the occasion and indifferent to the policemen.

'You were terrific,' Peterman said, to start them off.

Matera glanced at them. 'Yeah? I was hired to play a stooge. This is a nice little break for me.' He looked down the auditorium to the back of the theatre and waved.

He gave off an air of simplicity, a lack of curiosity that indicated a complete absorption in himself, which was probably why he had been adequate for the role of sister's husband. The audience could tell at a glance that he was not comic relief, and that he would not be involved in any downstage confrontations. At most he would be left to pick up the pieces by holding his crying wife after the family had fought it out. But he managed well enough in his new rôle of the hero's brother who has grown up in his sibling's shadow.

'Did you know Hunter well?' Salter asked.

'I don't think I spoke to the guy twice. I heard all about him when he was at Brighton last year, in the summer theatre, and what I heard didn't grab me. But he kept his distance. There was a lot of gossip about him—women, gambling—you probably already know. He made a pass at everything around here.'

'Including Granny?' Peterman asked delightedly.

Matera looked at Peterman until the policeman stopped smiling. 'The name is Penny Wicklow. Yes, her, too. Just once.'

'Jesus.'

This tidbit apart, they were getting the same gossip now from everyone. 'Let's call it a day,' Salter said, when Matera had left.

'We should talk to Granny.'

'Why?'

'I want to get a look at her.'

GRANNY SATISFIED Peterman's curiosity immediately. Under the grey make-up she was an attractive forty, flat-chested, tall, but otherwise with the figure of the leader of an aerobics class. Peterman congratulated her on her convincing portrayal of an eighty-year-old.

'It's my specialty,' she said. 'I wasn't getting anywhere playing Hedda Gabler. There's something about me that makes people laugh. And there was a shortage of old women so I made a study of them.' She let her body sag slightly, a hump appeared between her shoulders and her eyes moved back and forth between the two men. She was the Aged P., the listener in the corner, ready to come in with the shrewd/comic/sour/vulgar-but-licensed-by-her-age, or even, in revivals, wise remark that precedes the curtain. 'It cuts down on my height, too,' she added.

'That's terrific,' Peterman said. 'Which one turned Hunter on, you or Granny?'

Wicklow laughed. 'Both, I would think.'

'Did he try real hard, or was it just a reflex? Did he care what you looked like?'

Salter, too, wanted to know if Hunter's behaviour had been enough to give Wicklow a grudge against him, but it would have taken him several questions to get to the point reached by Peterman.

Wicklow said, 'Didn't you hear the details? OK, I'll tell you. There was just one try. What everyone heard was me, in bell-like tones, saying, "Son, I ain't opened my legs on request for thirty years, so take your hand

off my ass and let me get on with my work." That
stopped him, because for all he knew Connie Spurling was around somewhere. She usually was. I wanted
to let him know that it would happen every time he
tried. And put a label on him for the benefit of those
student ushers who might have been impressed by
him.'

'You worked with him before?' Salter asked.

'I met him at Brighton last summer.'

'So, you knew what he was like?'

'Oh, sure, but for the last little while he'd behaved
himself. While Connie Spurling was around.'

Salter stood up and walked to the edge of the dais.

'Anybody else know him better than you?' Peterman asked.

'Bill Turgeon. He was with him at Brighton last
summer, a stage-hand or something. I think Hunter
got him the job here.'

'That's enough,' Salter said. 'Tell the others to leave
their addresses and phone numbers, too, before they
go.'

'We should talk to this Turgeon guy,' Peterman
said.

'I already did. He wasn't much help. We'll come
back if we have to.'

When the two policemen were alone, Salter said,
'Tomorrow I'll check with Inspector Corelli again. See
if he's heard anything more.'

'Then?'

'I don't know. Go on leave. Let you look after it.
What do you guys do when you're sure it's the mob?'

'Hand it over to the organized crime unit, let the Mounties have a share, and the provincial police.'

'Then?'

'Get on with something else.'

'That sounds like a good idea.'

TEN

'I'LL HAVE TO STAY to get them settled, Charlie.'

Annie, on the phone from Prince Edward Island, had just finished explaining that her father was now permanently installed in a nursing home and was unlikely to recover enough to be taken home, and that she was trying to get her mother to decide what to do with herself.

'What are the options? What about your brothers?'

Both of Annie's brothers lived on the Island, operating different parts of the family businesses which included a resort hotel, two gas stations and a real estate company.

Salter continued, 'I just read this article in the paper about how men have got to learn to be more nurturing, because most old people are women so the old men are surrounded by women, old dolls in the homes and young ones doing the nursing, but what they need is caring men. Your father needs his sons to nurture him, not you.'

'It's Mother who's the problem. She won't hear of burdening the boys. She wouldn't move in with either one of them, even if they begged her, which they haven't. She says she wouldn't be comfortable. She's right, she wouldn't, because her daughters-in-law wouldn't allow her to take over.'

'Can't she stay alone? Your dad had a stroke, not her.'

'I don't think so. Before Dad had the stroke he was doing most of the cooking, because it's getting hard for her to function in a kitchen with her arthritis. Not that she ever liked cooking much.'

'She still plays golf! So what's the answer! A home? Is there a good one on the Island.'

'Several. But when I mentioned it she started to cry.'

'What, then?'

Annie didn't reply.

'Us? Have her here? Why is that better than her living with her sons?'

'Because I'm her daughter. She wouldn't feel out of place in my house.'

'She would in mine.'

'Don't shout at me, Charlie. I'm having a rough time. That's not what she had in mind, anyway.'

'Good. What, then?'

'You might as well hear it. She doesn't want to move away from her grandchildren here, and she doesn't want to be a burden on her sons, because they have their own problems with the business and their families.'

'So?'

Annie took a deep breath. 'This afternoon she thought again how nice it would be if the boys could find you a suitable position in the business, and you could take early retirement and we could move down here and she could help us set up a home.'

It had been coming for a long time and now that the brake of her husband was gone, Annie's mother could no longer restrain herself from betraying how she felt about having a policeman for a son-in-law compared to her Island tycoons of sons, a man, moreover, who had repeatedly been offered a place in the family business, but who insisted on chasing thieves and murderers for a living.

'I see. We mustn't upset the golden boys, but I'm supposed to jump at the chance to be a real member of the family at last and become respectable.'

'Don't shout at me, Charlie. I'm just trying to let you now what I have to cope with.'

'What did you say to her?'

'Nothing. I'm trying to make it clear that the idea isn't worth considering. You know how it is. I don't want to get into an argument. There's only one answer—no. But if I ever suggest any reasons then she'll meet all the arguments and I'll finish up defending myself. She hasn't actually suggested it, and I'm not picking up any hints.'

'What about your brothers? Do they agree with her?'

'They're leaving me to sort it out with Mother.'

'That's very decent of them. Don't take sides, eh? Because they fucking well think that it's a reasonable possibility? Well, I'll tell you what to do. Tell them I've discovered I'm allergic to potatoes, that it's more than my sinuses are worth to go within a mile of a potato field. Oh, what the hell. Can't you just hire someone to live with her?'

'She doesn't like the idea of a stranger in the house.'

'Nor do I.'

'I'll call you tomorrow. How are you getting on?'

'We're fine. Seth's play starts tomorrow. He's nice to live with. Worries I might get lonely if he goes out. And he misses you.'

'I miss him, tell him. And you.'

'Don't let them load it on you, Annie.'

'I won't. All I'm doing is telling you what's happening. so let me talk. Don't shout at me.'

THE NEXT MORNING he was called into the deputy chief's office. Inspector Corelli was already there.

Mackenzie waited for Salter to sit down, waited some more to create a little drama, then picked up the newspaper from his desk and waved it in the air. 'Seen this?'

Salter nodded. 'This' was a front page article saying that the police were again concentrating their search for the killer on the Italian community. It was larded with quotes from Salter suggesting that the community knew the killer and was hiding him. The article ended with a direction to an editorial. The editorial deplored Salter's racism, spent some time on the contribution of the Italians to the community, and ended by suggesting that Salter's own racial roots were too common among Metro's finest, and that the police commission needed to look closely at their hiring policies which did not reflect the richness of the city's mosaic.

'I thought it would be stronger than that,' Salter said.

Mackenzie laid the article on his desk and leaned back. 'What the bloody hell are you up to?'

'Had any reaction yet?'

'You mean apart from a phone call from the chief at six-thirty this morning, and calls from every other newspaper in town?'

Salter shrugged and waited. He had guessed why Corelli was there.

The deputy nodded to Corelli.

'I got a call from a good source,' Corelli said.

'The mob have put out a contract on Hunter's killer,' the deputy said.

Corelli looked pained, and slightly irritated at having his line stolen. 'Not quite,' he said.

'Isn't that what it is? A contract?'

'It could turn into one, but you need a name to put on a contract. What they've done is put up a little reward money for information.'

'You hear that?' the deputy asked Salter. 'You hear that? They're posting fucking rewards now. You'd better find this guy before they do, Salter, or we'll wind up looking very stupid. They've got a whole justice system running parallel to ours. Difference is, they've still got the death penalty.'

'How much?'

'I heard fifty grand,' Corelli said.

Salter was impressed. 'This thing started with just a thousand. What are they saying?'

'They are saying that it's not them and they want us to understand that.'

'So it's not them officially, but it could still be one of their collectors who went too far.'

Corelli thought about this and shook his head. 'Same thing. I'd assume it's not them in any way. They don't have anyone on their payroll that fits the description. They're upset. It's bad for business if civilians like Hunter get killed in their name. The politicians won't want their money come election time.'

'Sounds like the goods, Salter,' the deputy warned.

Salter agreed. 'I think we can forget about them now. Look somewhere else.'

'You realized the reaction you would get? *I* would get?'

'Oh, sure. But I couldn't see a quicker way to finding out what we needed to know to cut down the scope of the inquiry.'

'What have you found out?'

'The mob isn't involved. I believe that now. We could put out a statement that we have now satisfied ourselves that this is not a gang-related killing.'

'We'll do no such fucking thing. You know what the headline would be? "Mob tells cops to lay off", or some such.' Now that he understood, the deputy slumped back in his chair. 'I guess you've found out something, but you sure as hell haven't done yourself any good. People remember these things.'

You're the people, Salter thought. So I won't get to be deputy.

'Where else have you looked?' the deputy asked. Before Salter could answer, he added, 'Thanks, Sam,' and Corelli left.

Salter closed the door behind him. 'If it isn't the mob, then it's one of the independents. So far the message is negative there, too, though.' He recounted the substance of his meeting with the bookie, Taber.

'So I'm looking for a bookie that Taber doesn't know, or it's just personal.'

'Someone in the theatre business? Would they really kill for a part?' Mackenzie smiled slightly to show he knew the phrase.

'It's a possibility, but I don't think so.' Salter recounted the interviews he had conducted with some of the cast. 'Nobody liked Hunter, but we didn't get a smell of anxiety.'

'Get going, then. We've had two editorials so far. There'll soon be a special two-part article about famous unsolved cases. No ideas at all?'

'Just one I have to clean up. The guy was certainly a compulsive gambler, by all accounts. The people close to him in the play last summer noticed it towards the end of last season. So I'm taking a run down to talk to the people in the town he was playing. Some kind of summer theatre, like Niagara-on-the-Lake. See, all the information I'm getting is about Toronto, but Hunter might have been settling an old debt, one he made with a bookie out of town. I'm going to try to find out who you bet with down there.'

'You still working with Peterman?'

'He's got a couple of other cases, but I have him when I need him. I'd better get going.'

'Talked to Horvarth yet?' the deputy said, as Salter reached the door.

'Yesterday.'

'And?'

'He's all ready for a formal inquiry. I tried to frighten him a little. No dice.'

'Did you get *anything* off him?'

'I think he wants to go down fighting. Those pictures are pretty conclusive, but they didn't shake him as much as I thought they would. He wants to know who took them.'

'Did you tell him?'

'No, and when I didn't, that's when he clammed up again. As far as I can tell, he thinks if you and he get together in your office, you'll fix it so that he doesn't suffer too much, ask for his resignation and burn the pictures, maybe, but then he'll never know who set him up.' As he spoke it became clear to Salter that he was on the right track. 'He wants to see the whites of their eyes.'

'Does he think it was one of his own guys? Lindstrom, maybe?'

'I think that's exactly what he thinks.'

'Come back and sit down, Salter. What do I do?'

'Will the Mounties go along with an informal meeting?'

'They'll be suspicious as hell. It's the beginning of a cover-up. I'll be out in a minute,' he ended, shouting savagely at someone opening the door.

'Horvarth's entitled to know what the evidence is, isn't he?'

'In law, probably. I'll ask our lawyers. But I'm trying to avoid that.'

'If Horvarth is guaranteed that the guy who took the pictures will be there, he might come. I don't know. Maybe you could assemble an inquiry, then stop it as soon as it's obvious you're going to have to go public. I'm out of my depth. I was never a deputy in the old days.'

Mackenzie got up and walked to the door, opened it, and closed it again. 'It's not as if it's just the pictures. This guy is prepared to testify that he saw Horvarth taking money off someone another time, at Greenwood in April.'

'Christ. Then if the evidence is that solid it doesn't matter if Horvarth knows it, does it? He'd be entitled to know before he comes up before a public tribunal.'

'Tell him,' Mackenzie said suddenly, speaking to the window, 'tell him.'

'That it's the Mounties?'

'No. Tell him that we've got evidence that he took money earlier.' He crossed to his desk and took a sheet of paper from a folder. 'April twelfth, at Greenwood. Maybe when he hears that, he'll talk to me. I'll have another word with the Mounties.'

SALTER SPENT HALF AN HOUR with Peterman before he left. Peterman said, 'Mob or not, it's still gamblers. We've had it from too many people that he was mixed up with them and from Connie Spurling that he had the money to pay them off.'

'I'm trying to narrow down the gamblers. Anything else?'

'Find out what we can about Hunter.'

'Maybe I can pick something up in Brighton. Anything else?'

'Women.'

'Then why did he take a thousand dollars along?'

'Jesus. How do I know? I'm just feeding you lines here. Maybe it's the Chicago connection. Maybe the guy in Chicago has been dealing under the counter with Hunter and Spurling—they offered him a thousand for himself if he would take Hunter to Chicago. He meets Hunter at the motel, kills him, and keeps the bribe. Connie Spurling knows this but she can't tell us because she knows who he was meeting at the motel—she set it up—but it's a scuzzy deal so she would be finished as an agent if anyone found out. The guy from Chicago has a gold tooth by the way. How's that?'

'Terrific. But it should all come out in the last chapter. I'll talk to you when I get back from Niagara.'

PETERMAN'S NONSENSE about a 'Chicago connection' reminded him to talk again with the crying girl that Spurling had fired.

He found her at home, in a flat she shared with two other girls on Howland Avenue. 'I was just driving by and I thought I'd check to see if you had any problems,' he said.

'Not really. She says she's not going to pay me for the last two weeks but I don't care, so long as she leaves me alone.'

'Any sign of another job?'

'It's only been a day. I'm not looking properly yet.'

'Can I come in for a minute?'

'Sure.' She opened the door wide. 'Shall I make you a cup of coffee?'

'No, no. I just thought you might be able to tell me something about Hunter's background.'

'I don't want anything to do with anything connected with her.'

'I won't tell her.' He sat on a straight-backed chair as she perched on the edge of a couch opposite.

'You must have read the papers,' he said. 'They all say that Hunter was killed because of something to do with gambling.'

'The Mafia, they say.'

'We aren't sure. Did you ever see any sign of anyone suspicious, like not the sort of person you'd expect to see around a theatre?'

'A gangster, you mean?'

'All right, a gangster.' One with an Italian accent, about five feet eleven with a gold tooth.

She shook her head. 'Nobody like that.'

'When was the last time the manager from Chicago called?'

'Chicago? Oh God, yes. Last week. She was calling him in Chicago three times a day. Once she and Mr Hunter had a shouting match about it.'

'About what?'

'This Chicago thing. I don't know. But she was phoning him, the man from Chicago, right up until that weekend. Actually *they* had a shouting match, too. Well, she did the shouting.'

'You remember any of it?'

'I remember she was telling him not to be chicken. Don't be chicken, she said.'

It was the kind of phrase that would fit into several different scenarios. Useless. Feeling slightly foolish, Salter asked, 'Did you ever see the man from Chicago?'

'Just once. She was furious about that, too. I didn't know who he was so I was taking his name and asking him if I could tell her what he wanted to see her for. I didn't know he had an appointment. She walked in and overheard me and sort of grabbed him and took him into her office and afterwards she told me that I should have looked in *her* appointment book and that I had no business cross-questioning him in the office where we could be overheard. But how was I to know? His name wasn't in *my* book. He was just a voice on the phone to me.'

'What did he look like?'

'Sort of short, stocky. Bald. Quite old. About fifty.'

Finally Salter asked, 'After Mr Hunter left the play, did anyone connected with it come to see her?'

'Mr Adler came once, but she had me tell him she wasn't in. And the stage manager. He came in the day after Mr Hunter was killed, but she didn't even let him into the office. She told me to tell him that she wanted to be left alone. She was so rude sometimes. He could *see* her sitting in her office telling me to tell him to go away.'

HE DROVE OUT to Glencairn Avenue and passed on the message to Horvarth.

Horvarth said, 'When did I commit this first offence?'

'April twelfth. Greenwood.'

'Can you hang on a minute?' Horvarth ran up the stairs to a room above.

When he came back, a long minute later, he was talking as he came down the stairs. 'All right. Call it what you like—formal, informal, whatever. I'll come if the guy who took the pictures is going to be there.'

'Mackenzie didn't guarantee that he would be.'

'That's the thing that matters to me. If he comes, I'll come.'

'I'll tell him. This is just you and me talking, Joe. You understand?'

'I understand. Mackenzie's been informed of evidence against me, and he's sent me on leave with instructions not to talk to anyone. So I haven't. Don't worry about that. Does Internal Affairs know?'

Internal Affairs was the unit that would have to pick up the case if it went any further.

'Not as far as I know.'

'Then if Mac can produce this guy, we might be able to settle it his way.'

ELEVEN

LIKE ALL TORONTONIANS, Salter never visited Niagara Falls if he could avoid it because of the many times when he could not avoid it. House guests, especially visitors from the United States and Europe, generally have the Falls on the top of their list of things to see and do around Toronto, and Salter usually chauffeured guests to see it at least once a year. But it occurred to him as he was driving down the Queen Elizabeth Way that he had not been for two years, and never just for the fun of it, on his own.

The Falls look more spectacular in the movies, but on the other hand, the slight diminution of grandeur is made up for by the pleasurable shock of recognition, for the first two or three minutes. After that the visitor may walk under the Falls, and, if he or she is still not satisfied, take the boat cruise to within soaking distance of the spray. And that is it. The area is maintained by a Parks Commission which does a fine job of keeping tackiness at bay. On the Canadian side, the river bank for the whole viewing distance is maintained as a park with only the most inoffensive government buildings selling souvenirs and meals. All the commercial development is kept out of sight, in the town, and it is easy to ignore it or find it depending on the visitor's taste.

Salter generally took his guests directly to the Falls, about an hour-and-a-half's drive on a weekday, walked them up and down a bit to get them slightly damp from the spray, then carted them off to Niagara-on-the-Lake. There were several reasons for this. First of all there is only one restaurant at the Falls itself, the Parks' concession, and it is always full. Secondly, the drive from Niagara Falls through to Niagara-on-the-Lake is through parkland and past fruit farms where you can buy the best peaches the peninsula has to offer. And if the guests were curious to sample Canadian wine, Salter took them to the Inniskillen vineyards where he could surprise them with the discovery that the ice wine made there is the best and the most expensive in the world. Lastly Salter could count on his guests being pleased by the preserved nineteenth-century look of Niagara-on-the-Lake, with its quaint storefronts, the mob-caps on the help, and the horehound candy in every other window. It was always a pleasant place to spend an hour and besides, there are restaurants there for every taste; good, indifferent, and bad.

Salter left Horvarth at ten, meaning to head directly for Brighton, but an hour-and-a-half later found him parked at the Falls for the first time that year, a tourist in his own back yard. The Falls were still there, and after five minutes Salter drove on to Brighton.

The sergeant on duty at the Brighton police station had been expecting Salter for an hour. 'You called before nine. Said you were on your way. It's—' he looked at his wrist—'half eleven. You should've been here by half ten.'

'I had a look at the Falls.'

'Ho,' the sergeant said, or rather, shouted, with a noise like a small balloon bursting. 'That right? I see. Bring your camera, did you?'

He does it well, Salter thought. It was impossible to tell if the sergeant was bucolic by nature or if he was managing a beautifully-poised bit of mockery directed at the rubber-necking of a Toronto staff inspector. To be certain, you needed to see the expression on the face of a third person in the room, someone who knew the sergeant well. 'I just wanted to see if they were still there.' He extended his hand.

'Of course. Where are my manners?' The sergeant flung himself forward across the desk to wring Salter's hand in what Salter was almost sure was a parody of goodwill and apology for not having shaken hands immediately. 'Brock,' he said. 'Jim Brock. Sergeant Jim Brock. And you are Staff Inspector...?'

'Charlie Salter.'

'You are indeed. And you've seen the Falls so we can get right to work. No need to waste any more time. Homicide, you say. How does it touch us?'

'The man who was killed was an actor. He was playing here last season. He seems to have been paying off a gambling debt when he was garrotted.'

Brock, who had been putting on a show of listening carefully, jumped slightly, looked around the room and stared offendedly at Salter, like a maiden aunt tracking down the perpetrator of a rude noise. 'Nothing to do with us, I should think. We don't go in for garrotting in Brighton. We use bits of wood and bottles.'

'We can't find any connection to the gambling scene in Toronto, and since he was gambling while he was here, I wondered if he still had debts that he hadn't left behind.'

'How much?'

'We think he had a thousand on him when he was murdered.'

'That's a lot of money. To us, I mean. Here. In Brighton.'

'It isn't enough to interest the mob.'

Once again Brock jumped in mock alarm. 'Let's keep those gentlemen out of it.'

'Don't they come down this way?'

'Not that I'm aware of. They come up as far as Niagara Falls through the Buffalo connection, I hear, but there are no pickings in a town of this size, thank God.'

'Do you have any independent bookies?'

'Again, not that I'm aware of. This is a holiday town.'

Salter had expected nothing different. Turgeon, the stage manager, had already said as much. 'So, if a gambling actor came to town, how would he get a bet on?'

'By phone to Toronto. Or he could drive over to Fort Erie. Half an hour, if he doesn't stop to look at the Falls.' Brock roared with laughter, now clearly mimicking a rural comedian, laughing at his own joke.

The door opened and a uniformed constable put his head through the crack. 'Sarge. A blue Chevy, parked behind the station. Know who owns it?'

Brock rose from his chair in genuine alarm, all the bufoonery draining away. 'That's mine. You know fucking well it is. Why?'

'Ray Hampton just smashed into it.' The face, glowing with the fun it was having, disappeared.

'Hampton?' He walked round the desk and past Salter. 'Smashed into it?' He passed through the door. 'My new car? Again?'

Salter heard him go through the station house and fade into the distance. 'My car?' he repeated, in the distance. 'My new car!'

The head reappeared. 'Sorry, sir. He just got it back from the shop. Hambone smashed into it last week, too.'

'Who's Hambone?'

'He's a new cadet. Sarge is very proud of that car.' The head grinned, and disappeared.

Salter waited a few minutes, but Brock had obviously forgotten all about him. He had most of what he came for and he guessed that if Brock ever returned he would not want to chat further that day, except about his car, so he wrote a note of thanks and asked the way to the theatre.

THERE ARE TWO important theatre festivals in southern Ontario, the Shakespeare Festival at Stratford and the Shaw at Niagara-on-the-Lake. The Brighton festival is a third. It has been running for several years, supported by the town council to attract tourists, to

persuade them to stay the night at the local motels. It
is housed in an old courthouse, built around the turn
of the century when Brighton looked as if it was going to be bigger than it became. The building was given
to the town by the province, and leased to the theatre
company for a dollar a year. The King's Players, as
they called themselves, have worked out a mix of light
comedy and melodrama from the 'thirties' repertoire
which nearly fills the house, mainly with people who
have seen the plays before and find it comforting to
know there are still nice plays around.

Salter had called ahead and the manager was waiting for him in his office. Salter explained his mission.

'I heard about that,' the manager said. 'Not nice.'

'Were you surprised?'

'Oh, sure. We talked about it around here. We had
no idea he was in so deeply. You hear of things like
that, of course, but you don't meet many gambling
actors. Mostly, when an actor gets into trouble, it's
sex, drugs or professional jealousy. There's a lot of
emotion in this business and you get some vicious in-
fighting sometimes. Nearly all of it is verbal, though.
Being killed for a gambling debt is a new one to me.'

'What makes you think it was a gambling debt?'

'Wasn't it? We heard it was the Mafia.' The manager became defensive. 'That's what everyone says.'

'You ever see any suspicious-looking strangers
hanging around the stage door, looking for him?'

'Well, no, but . . . he did go to the races a lot.'

'Did he?' Salter leaned forward. 'Did he tell you
that?'

'No, but ... actually, yes, he did. Every spare after-noon while they were running at some track nearby.'

'Fort Erie?'

'Is that the place?' The manager found another de-tail for Salter. 'He used to brag a lot when he won.'

'Can you tell me anything else about him?'

The manager was slightly on the defensive, not wanting Salter to turn a small gossipy remark into a major investigation. 'He was a good actor.'

'Was he gay?'

'No! For God's sake, is that the first thing you people think of? As a matter of fact, it was quite the opposite. If it hadn't been for that agent or spouse or whatever she is, he'd have screwed every female in the cast. And the cleaning staff, too.'

'Is that right?'

'You must know this already. Haven't you inter-viewed the cast of the play he was in?'

Salter pretended to muse. 'Oh, yeah, sure. But hearing you say it gives me an idea.'

'I didn't say anything you didn't know.'

'No, but I just realized something. He might have made a lot of enemies.'

'He did, but I don't know anyone who would have killed him.'

'That woman of his ... ?'

'Connie Spurling. Have you talked to her?'

'Just for a minute. She kept close tabs on him, did she?'

Now the manager was looking wary. If Salter was fishing, he didn't want to be his guide. 'More or less.'

'Look, I need to find out about all the possible enemies Hunter might have had. I will, too, sooner or
later. But if Connie Spurling kept such close tabs on
him, then it's unlikely I'll have to dig around among
the actors who were here last summer.'

'Right.' The manager nodded eagerly. 'Frankly, the
way she kept him from straying was something of a
joke. She drove down from Toronto just about every
night and waited for him after the performance. She
would stay the night with him and go back the next
morning. A classical recipe for keeping a husband
faithful.'

'Did she go to the races with him?'

'I don't think so, no. She let him off the leash for
that. She had to work, after all. He wasn't her only
client.'

'Did you find her a nuisance, hanging about backstage?'

'God, yes. I didn't dislike her, though,' he added
warningly.

'So the way you remember it, she made sure Hunter
behaved himself while he was here.'

The manager considered the implications for himself in admitting this much. Seeing none, he said, 'Yes,
that's the way it looked to me.' Then, just in case, he
added, 'Of course, I wasn't next to him all the time.
You'll have to get the view of the others.'

'Who were they?'

'Who?'

'The others. The other actors.'

The manager thought for a moment, then went to a
file and pulled out some theatre programmes and a

number of glossy photographs. 'These are the plays he was in.' He handed Salter the programmes. 'These pictures were taken for publicity.'

Salter scanned the cast lists, looking for familiar names. Finding two, he said, 'I suppose they are scattered across the country by now.'

The manager looked over the programmes. 'Hunter was the star. I couldn't tell you where the others are, except her.' He put his finger on the name of the costume designer.

'Where is she?'

'She committed suicide late in the summer.'

'Was there a story behind it?'

'Of course, but I don't know what it was. She was just found dead in her room. No note. Nothing. She just swallowed a lot of secobarb. First we knew of it, someone came running back from the house saying Mary had taken an overdose of secobarb. By the time I got to the hospital she had been pronounced dead.'

Something to check. 'And none of the rest were especially close to Hunter that you know? I mean like worth my taking a trip to Vancouver to interview them?'

'I told you, with Connie Spurling there wasn't room for anyone else, even if anyone had liked the man.'

Salter gathered the programmes and pictures together. 'I'll keep this lot for a while.'

'I want it all back. I'm starting an archive.'

'Just a temporary loan. Make a list and I'll give you a receipt.'

SERGEANT BROCK was still recovering. When Salter walked in Brock nodded at him, put the phone down and added one more to a list of figures which he then added up while Salter waited.

'Eighteen hundred and fifty plus,' he said. 'The whole rear end, the trunk and the back door. Then there's the paint job. The little bastard hit it *twice*. He smashed into the back, reversed, put it in first, decided to reverse a bit more, forgot he was in forward and smashed into the side. I've got a special price for fixing it from Minty's Garage. Eighteen hundred and fifty. Plus.'

'Was he driving a police car?'

'He was driving his pal's truck.'

'His insurance will go through the roof. So will yours.'

Brock got up, closed the door, sat down, leaned forward to look deep into Salter's eyes, and said, 'He wasn't insured.'

'The truck was. It had to be. You can't get a licence without insurance.'

'Yes, you can. The truck is a little runabout, like a reinforced golf cart. It's only licensed for use on a farm or vineyard. His pal didn't tell him.' Brock was getting some satisfaction out of laying out his disaster step by step.

'What are you going to do?'

'I've got two choices. Proceed formally and finish the kid and his pal for life. Or pay it myself and get it back at five dollars a week from the kid. I've only had the car three months and he's hit it twice, three times if you count two for today. If we get through this, I'm going to get that kid a pedal cycle. I'll have to talk to Minty's Garage some more.'

'Get them to sell you a load of angle iron.'

'What?'

'I learned to drive on a construction site out west. The day I got my licence, I backed a company truck into a wall. The foreman reamed me out for twenty minutes, then he drove into town and left the truck to be fixed. The garage did it for free, but a week later the company got a bill for five hundred feet of angle iron, and everyone was happy. We included the bill in the week's costs—it was a government contract, cost-plus—so we made money on the deal.'

'This how you operate in Toronto?'

'No, no. You have to be in a small way of business so that not too many people are involved. Out west.'

Now Brock showed he was recovering by smiling slightly. He looked out the window at the parking lot. 'Why would I buy angle iron?' He turned back to Salter. 'What did you come back for?'

'Mary Mikhail. Worked for a theatre last summer. Committed suicide. Was there a story?'

Brock pressed some buttons on a small computer and started to read. 'Mary Mikhail. Found without vital signs, two-thirty, August sixteenth. Taken to hospital. Resuscitation attempted. Pronounced dead at the hospital.'

'Who found her?'

'Sonia Lewis and Penny Wicklow. Both actresses.'

'Then what?'

'According to this, the two women walked over to her house because she hadn't appeared to do some work on their costumes. They found her, and sent for us and the medics. When we got there, the landlady had taken charge. She'd sent the two women downstairs to wait in the living-room and was guarding the bedroom door so no one else would wander in.'

'An overdose of secobarb, the theatre manager said.'

'That was the finding.'

'No note?'

'Not that we found. I read an article in the paper the other day, said that four out of five suicides go without leaving any message behind.'

'How many did she take?'

'The autopsy report says at least twenty.'

'Was she pregnant?'

'She was thirty-nine, and anyway, I don't think that's a reason these days. Her colleagues testified that she was manic depressive. One said she realized afterwards that she had been bad for some time. There was nothing to investigate.'

Brock wandered over to the window, returning to his main concern. 'I can't buy goddam angle iron,' he said.

'What else does the garage sell?'

'Firewood, coal, ice.' Then, 'Gravel,' he said. 'His brother sells gravel. How much does gravel cost? That parking lot's a mess.' Catching Salter's eye, he laughed. 'Just kidding,' he said.

But when Salter left, Brock already had the telephone directory in his hands, waiting for Salter to go away.

TWELVE

THERE WAS A PACKSACK in the hall and a large cloth bag of the kind professional tennis-players carry. On top of the bags was a down-filled parka. Salter walked through to the front of the house and found Seth in the kitchen, eating cereal. 'I have an early rehearsal,' Seth said. 'This'll keep me. I'll get a pizza after. I'm running low, though.'

Salter gave him twenty dollars. 'Where is he?' he asked.

'They came in and went out again.'

'They?'

'He brought a girl with him.'

'Anyone we know?'

'New one. They went out to buy groceries. She went through the cupboards and the fridge, but we don't have her kind of food.'

'What is she? Eskimo?'

'You mean Innuit. No. She's a cook. That's what she sounds like. They're cool. They don't spend all their time kissing.'

The door opened and Salter's elder son, Angus, came in, hugged his father briefly, then said this is Linda.

She put out her hand and Salter felt the long fingers coiling individually, earnestly around his palm, while she held up her head to be looked at. She was about Angus's age, he guessed, twenty or twenty-one, in a cotton sweater without a brassiere, and a pair of blue jeans, with sandals on small, pretty feet. Her face was spotty, and her hair was a big brown tangle and she had been unlucky with her teeth, which were grey—a childhood disease?—but on the whole Salter could see Angus's point.

'Why don't we save everything until I've got supper ready,' she said. Her voice was soft and light and heavily mannered, swooping up and down on every other word as if she had spent her whole life talking winningly to three-year-olds.

'Right,' Salter said. 'I'll make a drink. What would you like?'

'Beer,' Angus said.

'Wine, please. There's a bottle in the fridge,' Linda said.

Salter, slightly offended by the way in which this woman/child was taking over his/Annie's kitchen, and not very intrigued by her vocal style, yet recognized that Linda provoked lewd thoughts, and she could cook apparently: two big areas taken care of.

Seth finished his cereal and disappeared, and Salter decanted the drinks and took his into the living-room. He watched an old episode of *Golden Girls* for half an hour and had a shower so as not to appear to be waiting with his stomach growling, and then was called into the kitchen.

He feared that Linda would be vegetarian, or into bran or some such, and at first glance the table did look macrobiotic. There was a large salad with red lettuce and some sliced black bread and margarine instead of butter, but as he sat down Linda produced rice and a kind of curry stew whose main ingredients appeared to be chicken and peanuts. It was good food, as Salter quickly acknowledged, and he was just as impressed by the fact that Angus had clearly played an important if supporting part in producing it.

He was half prepared for what came next. After the ice-cream and coffee, after he had told Angus the latest news of his grandfather, after he had heard that Angus's year in business school had gone well, he said, 'I don't know if your bed's made up. Your mother left in a hurry, but you know where the sheets and stuff are.'

Linda started to clear the table, and Angus said, 'Linda and I are going to live together.'

'Here?' Salter said, just managing to stop himself saying, 'Not here, you're not.'

'Of course not. We're going to look for a place.'

'What with?' Salter asked, cursing himself for sounding immediately aggressive, trying to remind himself to talk to Angus as if he were the kid next door, politely, interestedly.

'We have enough to start with. Linda has her own furniture. And I'll get a job.'

It was no surprise. Angus had been sleeping with his girls ever since he had discovered them. And saving his money. Salter thought briefly about the difference between the two sons: Seth, the dreamer, transforming himself imaginatively every year, now to be an actor; and Angus, totally clearheaded, organizing his world to the best advantage, studying business, and now arranging a pleasant summer for himself. It was hard to remember now that Angus had once said he wanted to be an actor, when he was fourteen. Salter also thought briefly of the difference between Angus and himself at that age, only briefly because the comparison seemed all in Angus's favour. 'It seems like a lot of upheaval for just a few months.'

'I'm going to take a year off, Dad.'

Nothing new here. They all did it. Worn out at the age of eighteen or twenty-one, the children of the middle classes had, for at least a generation, taken a year off before they confronted life. What was odd was that the usual given reason was that the children were understood to be finding themselves in London or Paris, or, more lately, Japan, but Angus had been sure of himself since he was sixteen.

'You having doubts about your course?'

'Oh no. But I want to get out there, see what it's like.'

'In business.'

'Yeah.'

'Will anyone hire you without a degree?'

'If they don't, we'll start our own.'

'You have some ideas?'

'Lots,' Linda said, rejoining them.

As they talked, Salter set about cleansing his mind of assumptions, the chief of which was that this girl was in some remote way descended from the hippies who followed his own generation, an assumption he had made because of his previous assumption that she was probably devoted to natural foods, which, although proven entirely unfounded, persisted to flavour his succeeding attitudes. In fact, if he closed his eyes and just listened to them talk, it was clear that her individualism took the form of wanting to cut as many throats as fast as possible in pursuit of the good life.

The telephone rang, and it was Annie, and after exchanging their news and telling Annie who was with him, he handed the phone over to Angus, and moved with Linda to the living-room at the back of the house to give Angus some privacy, saying only, as he did so, 'Tell her.'

'Nice dinner,' he said to Linda.

'Just chemistry and timing.'

She's as confident as he is, Salter thought. 'Where will you look for a place? In the Beaches or the Annexe?' he asked, naming the two areas which he believed to be full of happily-unmarried couples living on the third floors of carved-up houses.

'Angus wants to live around here. Perhaps a little farther south, so we won't need two cars.'

After a bit more of this, Angus called from the kitchen. 'Mum wants to speak to you,' he said.

Salter picked up the phone having no idea what Annie's reaction would be. 'I've suggested to him that he bring her down here for a holiday before they set up house,' she said immediately. 'I'd like to get a look at her, and his grandmother will be thrilled to bits. It'll take some of the weight off me. What do you think?'

But Salter had no idea what to think. He felt as if he were in a play in which everyone knew their lines except him. So he reverted to type, 'You going to put them in the same bedroom?' he asked, assuming the question was rhetorical in the house of an eighty-year-old-Prince-Edward-Island-matriarch.

'I'll have to think about that.'

'Did he say yes?'

'Ask him, will you? He had to ask his girl.'

Salter leaned towards the living-room holding up the phone. Angus said, 'Tell her, yes. But we'll come by train. Linda has never taken that trip.' He walked to the kitchen and took the phone off Salter. 'We'll come by train, Mum. If we leave tomorrow morning we'll be there the day after. Can you meet us? Great.' He waggled the phone at Salter who shook his head, said 'Bye, Mum,' and hung up.

Salter said, 'What about tonight?'

Linda said, 'I'm staying with my sister tonight.'

Salter searched for and found a flaw. 'What about your laundry?' He nodded in the direction of Angus's bags. 'You won't have time to do it.'

'We did it before we left Western. We're all set.'

I guess you are, Salter thought. If you were the kid next door I'd be really impressed, so why do I feel sad?

THIRTEEN

'IT'S THIS GHOST BOOKMAKER that interests me,' Salter said to Peterman the next day. 'There aren't any bookies in Brighton. I think I'm going to take a run down to the local track and poke around a little.'

'It's supposed to be sunny all day,' Peterman said.

Salter almost coloured. The need to look at Fort Erie racetrack, had, in fact, coincided in his mind with the idea of another kind of outing.

He closed the door of his office and dialled the number of the Chelsea Inn. 'How about coming to the races with me? A day out. We'll go through Niagara Falls, if you like.'

'Don't be silly. I'm here to work.'

'I could postpone until tomorrow. When does the conference end?'

'It's over, I was planning to leave tomorrow, and I have some shopping to do today. As well as work.'

'Shop tonight. The Eaton Centre's open until nine. Come to the races.'

'I don't go to the races.'

'You've never been, you mean. Now's the time to start. I'll pick you up at nine-thirty, outside the hotel.'

'No, you won't.'

'Why? Afraid you might be seen getting into a car with a stranger?'

'Of course not. I told you, I have things to do.'

'Like what?'

'Where are these races?'

'Fort Erie. You won't know a soul. All gamblers and bookies and mobsters. But Niagara Falls will be your cover story.'

'Oh, stop it. All right. I'll come to your damn races. But I have to do a couple of errands first. Meet me somewhere.'

Salter laughed, on a roll. 'Anywhere you say. Where are the errands? Nothing's open yet.'

'I have to pick up a night school calendar from Douglas College. I'll walk over. I should be finished by nine-thirty.'

'Do you know Douglas College?'

'No.'

'I do. When you've got your calendar, ask someone where the bookstore is. I'll pick you up there at nine-thirty. Wear a big coat and dark glasses. I'll use my own car, a blue Jetta.'

'You're really enjoying yourself, aren't you?'

SHE WAS WAITING at the kerb, reading a newspaper like someone who is regularly given a lift from this spot at this time.

Salter pulled up and swung the door open. 'Scrunch down,' he said. 'This area is lousy with visitors from Ottawa.'

'One more,' she warned, 'and I'll get out at the next light.'

Salter looked at her, grinning. 'You look terrific,' he said and made to pat her knee.

'That's it. Stop the car. Come on, stop the car.'

'I'll keep my hands on the table,' Salter said. 'I promise.' He started to hum. 'Isn't it a great day?'

'You back to normal?'

'Nearly.'

'Good. Stay the way you are.'

Salter held up both hands briefly in an 'I surrender' gesture.

'Keep your hands on the wheel. That's good enough.'

They said nothing until they were well on to the Queen Elizabeth Way, passing Oakville.

'So tell me the rest of your life story,' Salter said. 'Otherwise we'll have to listen to *Morningside*.'

'Let's see. My earliest memory is of a boy in first year university who put his hand up my skirt. He pretended to be joking.'

'That wrist still hurts in cold weather.'

'Then I transferred to McGill where I met my husband. After six years I married him and moved to the University of Wisconsin where he did his Ph.D. Then we moved to Saskatoon, and then to Ottawa where he is now a dean so we'll probably stay there.'

'That's *his* life story. What about yours?'

'After I got married, it was the same thing.'

'And that's it?'

'I have a degree in chemistry and one in social work which I have never used except in volunteer work. Now what about you? How did you wind up in the police?' She had dropped the bantering tone of their previous encounter. 'Right. You told me. You were playing hockey and it seemed like a good idea at the time. And that's it?'

'Dull, isn't it?'

'I don't know. I haven't met your wife.'

Salter said nothing.

'You're obviously happy.'

'The older I get the more I'm glad to go home nights.'

'No regrets?' she asked, but not in a searching way.

'Oh, sure. "The Road Not Taken." Remember? Have you ever thought, I mean have you thought in the last couple of days that if it hadn't been 1957 we might have become lovers. They're all doing it now. They have dispensers in the washrooms.'

'Everybody's thought about that. Ever since the Beatles. Phillip Larkin wrote a poem about it.'

'You think it puts a gap between us and our kids?'

'My daughter says our generation is obsessed with sex. At least, her professors are. She's at Queen's.'

'Obsessed is strong. Preoccupied, maybe.'

Some of the traffic left them to go to Hamilton. 'We were the odds and sods. There was me, the missionary's daughter . . .'

'And me, the kid from Cabbagetown . . .'

'And Izzy. Remember him? What was he doing in Victoria College?'

'Trying to get away from his background, like the rest of us,' Salter said.

'That true?'

'Except for you, what we had in common was that college was a big let-down. You were slumming, trying not to conform to type, but the rest of us were homeless. Not one of them came back in second year, except me, and I only lasted four months. Izzy became a prison visitor or some such. I've seen him at the Don Jail.'

'I wasn't slumming. You're right, though. I was trying to avoid sororities and the Junior league.'

'And you've wound up right in the middle of it?'

'And who did you marry? The girl who ran the snack bar in Woolworth's in Cabbagetown?'

'Easy. That's not nice. She's like you—private school, old money, all that stuff.'

'Rosedale?' The home of the Establishment.

'Prince Edward Island's equivalent, yes.'

They finished the drive into Niagara Falls talking about their children.

In the event, she was not very interested in the Falls, either, and after five minutes of leaning over the rail, getting damp, they took the road again to Brighton. There he pulled up outside the police station without explanation and left her in the car while he went inside, returning to her raised eyebrows.

'Didn't I tell you I was working?' he said.

'Does he know you?' She looked in the direction of the station house. Sergeant Brock had accompanied Salter to the door.

'He doesn't know my wife. Quit worrying. I told you, scrunch down.'

'Did you tell him I was your wife?'

'I told him you were a colleague in drag.'

SALTER LED HER through the turnstiles at Fort Erie and up into the clubhouse. On the way he bought two programmes and gave her one which she stuffed into her purse without looking at it.

'You've really never been to the races before?' he asked.

She shook her head and smiled brightly at the world around her. It was the expression she would have adopted for a tour of the brothel district of Marrakech.

'There's nothing to it.' He opened his programme. 'See. Ten races. You pick a horse you like and I'll put a bet on for you.'

'I'll just watch.'

'Suit yourself. We have time for a hot-dog before the first race.'

She stood up immediately, and they found their way to the snack bar. After a hot-dog and a Coke, she stopped looking around her quite so brightly, and Salter tried to see what she was seeing.

'A lot of people are taking the day off,' he said.

'When we passed the betting windows, I saw a man bet a hundred dollars. He looked as if he was on welfare, but he had a hundred-dollar bill.'

'I gave up wondering about that a long time ago. Some people like to bet. They have jobs and they save up all their spare money to bet with. They don't own cars or buy clothes or go on vacations. They just bet.'

'That's awful.'

'There are degrees, I guess. Most of them take care of their lives first, then bet what's left over. Then there are the ones who regard two dollars spent on socks as a waste, a bet they didn't have. It's an addiction. You can get it bad, or you can keep it under control, like bridge. You play bridge? Let's go watch the first race.'

She pointed to the row of betting windows. 'Do those signs mean that Americans and Canadians have to bet at different places? How can they tell? Do you have to show a passport?'

'It's the money they care about, not your nationality. Those signs say what kind of money they take at the different windows. Saves a lot of making change. There are more people here from Buffalo than there are from Toronto.'

They walked through the clubhouse and looked at the track.

'Are all racetracks like this? It's so pretty!'

'It's said to be the prettiest racetrack in North America, but I imagine there's competition for that title.'

He had expected that she would bet two dollars to place under his direction, and win, maybe, fifty cents, but she kept her hand firmly clasped on her purse. 'I'll just watch.'

Salter put ten dollars on the favourite and lost.

She said, 'It's like throwing money into the gutter.'

'I might have won.'

'But you didn't. Ten dollars gone, just like that. How can you stand it?'

'I just can't help myself. Now I have to go to work. Will you be OK for a couple of races?'

'I brought a book.' She dug down into her purse and waved a paperback at him. As far as she was concerned the racetrack might have been a public park with some incomprehensible activity like bocci taking place in the middle distance.

'You'll be safe here.' Salter felt a joke coming on. 'No one was ever molested at the races. These people have one-track minds.'

'Oh, go and do your business. Then let's go.'

SALTER IDENTIFIED HIMSELF to the young security guard at the turnstiles who looked at the picture Salter showed him and handed it back immediately. 'Sorry. There's no way I could tell you if he came around last season. The regular guard is sick. I'm just filling in.'

'He came here pretty often, I'm sure. He's an actor.'

'Hang on.' The guard walked over to the turnstiles with Salter close behind and showed the picture to a girl sitting in one of the glass booths. 'Know him?' he asked. 'He's an actor.'

The girl, who had been watching and listening, shook her head. 'Tell him to try Joe Euringer.'

'Who's Joe Euringer?'

'He knows everybody. He used to do theatre publicity, and he likes horses. He's here. I spoke to him.'

'He could be anywhere by now, though.'

The girl looked up at the clock. 'He'll be in the paddock. He's one of the owners of a horse running this afternoon. He told me to bet on it. Got a programme? We're all sold out.'

Salter handed her his and she thumbed through it. 'Bird Watcher,' she said. 'Next race.'

'What's he look like?'

'Ask anyone in the paddock.'

'You can't get in the paddock without a pass,' the guard said.

The girl laughed. 'Here,' she said, taking a strip of cardboard from a drawer, one of a bundle held by a rubber band. 'This'll get you in.' She looked across at the guard. 'He's a policeman,' she said in the tone of someone talking to a backward ten-year-old. 'Conducting an investigation.'

EURINGER WAS a cheerful-looking man dressed in a tweed jacket, red trousers, a yellow tie, highly-polished ox-blood loafers and a blue corduroy cap. Salter found him watching his horse being saddled, and as soon as he had explained his mission, Euringer took the policeman by the arm, led him to the paddock rail, said, 'Don't move, I'll be right back,' trotted back to his horse, patted it, the jockey and the trainer, then returned, led Salter away, parked him by the betting windows, made a bet, and took Salter up to a private box to watch the race. 'We're going to win with this sucker,' he said. 'Then I'm all yours.'

Ten minutes later, Bird Watcher floated free at the turn and came home two lengths ahead of the field. Euringer tipped his hat over his eyes and said, 'Six to one,' folded his hands over his stomach, turned to Salter and said, 'That's my day made. Now let me make yours.'

'Hunter,' Salter reminded him.

'Right. I knew him. I heard he was dead. Something to do with gambling, I heard, but I didn't believe it.'

'Why?'

'I met him at Stratford. I've been around theatre for ten years and I've bumped up against most of the actors. Everyone knows I'm at the track when I'm not working, but I never got a hint from him that he liked to bet.'

'According to my information, Hunter used to come here when he was playing at the Brighton summer theatre last year. That's the story. I'd like to confirm it. The guard by the turnstiles couldn't help.'

'Who put you on to me?'

'The girl in the booth.'

'My girl.'

'Ah.'

'I guess you're entitled to know. If Hunter came to Fort Erie last summer, then he must have come on the days I wasn't here which were very few. Look at it down there.' He pointed to the stands which were about a quarter full. 'It's never that crowded. I wouldn't have missed him. You heard he came often?'

'All the time.'

'No way.' Euringer shook his head decisively. 'Once, maybe. Twice, even. No more. Someone's been telling you stories. Or Hunter was.'

Salter liked what he saw of Euringer. Happy, ebullient even, but sensible. A man it was safe to try a small speculation on. 'Who was Hunter telling stories to?'

'Connie Spurling. You know her?'

'I've talked to her.'

'Sure you have. She came out once, looking for him. I think she was on the same kick. Came out to see if he was lying, made himself a little space by taking up racing.'

'What did she say when you told her he never came?'

'I didn't. Hunter was a prick, but I didn't like her, either, and us guys gotta stick together. I told her I didn't come to the races too much myself but I'd seen him around. In fact, I said, I thought I'd seen him that afternoon, but he usually left before the last couple of races. I offered to find her someone else who'd seen him, but she was satisfied. She didn't want me to think she was checking up on him. Just chatting, she said she was. Had a little time to spare so she thought she'd drop by and meet him. So we let it go. But he wasn't here, and I'd never seen him here, and I think he was up to his old tricks, and that, I decided, was her problem.'

'What was he up to?'

'He was screwing someone, bet your life. That's not just my guess, either. I saw him once, driving away from a motel between here and Brighton. He drove a clapped-out Jaguar which I recognized. It was him all right.'

'Alone?'

Euringer laughed. 'Someone in a headscarf and sunglasses, though if I'd seen who it was I probably wouldn't tell you. It could have been one of a dozen, any time I knew him.'

'Remember the name of the motel?'

Euringer shook his head. 'You couldn't see it from the highway. I think there was a sign, but that's all. I remember his car came out of the trees. He was a lucky sonofabitch, though.'

'Why?'

'She checked up on him on a Monday. Another day and she'd have caught him.' Seeing Salter's face, he laughed. 'Didn't you know? Fort Erie only operates four days a week.' He stood up and took out his wallet. 'I have to collect and get on the next race. Here's my card, if you want to follow this up, but you probably got what you came for. Now me for my moolah.'

'How much did you bet?'

'Two hundred. Stay for a race and I'll buy you a drink.'

Salter shook his head. 'I've got someone waiting for me.' He pointed down to where Julie was sitting alone in the stands, reading. 'She thinks betting is wicked. Thanks, and thank your girl for me.'

'I will.' He looked down at Julie. 'You should get yourself a new one. Someone who likes the gee-gees. Like mine.'

'HAD ENOUGH?'

She looked up and gave him her number one smile. 'Time to go?'

'If we leave now we can beat the rush.'

'Finished working?'

'Just about.' He led her along the stands and out to the paddock. He wanted to make an attempt to get her to see something of the magic which had cast a spell on him first in England, where he had been introduced to steeplechasing, and which was coming back to him now, making him promise himself that he would go out to Woodbine the first time Annie and the police gave him a day off. Julie had not been moved by the sight of thoroughbreds in motion. Perhaps a close-up would do it. 'Let's have a look at the line-up for the next race before we go.'

He led her to where the horses were circling to begin the walk to the post parade. 'Look at them,' he said. 'Aren't they beautiful?'

In fact the horses at Fort Erie are a modest lot during the week, racing for purses of four and five thousand, but to Salter's uneducated eye they seemed magnificent.

She was silent, and he thought he had her at last as she looked closely at every horse that passed. Then she turned at him, frowning. 'When do they put their spurs on?' she asked.

He took her arm and led her out through the turnstiles to the car. 'We'll go home along the shore.'

'You're in charge.'

He dawdled along looking for the right place, somewhere Hunter could have parked without being seen. The first two motels he came to were too close to the highway and all the parking spaces were in front.

'What are you looking for?'

'A motel you can't see from the highway. There!'

The sign pointing to the Frontier Motel drew him off the highway on to a short gravelled drive through a clump of trees to the slightly dilapidated motel building. Everything was being done to keep the motel bright; the paint was fresh, the grass cut, the stones besides the drive whitewashed, but the roof had been patched in a slightly different shade of tile, there were two wooden picnic tables instead of a pool, and the VACANCY sign looked permanent. It was probably cheap and clean but it was also old and promised nothing except a bed, and it obviously survived on the leftovers from the swankier motels they had passed.

There were no other cars behind the motel where the drive ended. Salter parked and jumped out of the car. 'Be right back,' he said.

Inside the office he found the man who was obviously the owner or his brother-in-law, a man in his seventies, standing behind the door, having watched Salter's arrival through the glass.

'On vacation?' he asked, reluctant to move behind the counter before he had had a chat. 'You folks are not from the States. I saw your licence plate. You're from Toronto. I guess you don't like to drive too far in a day. Where you heading?' He acted like a fellow guest, waiting for the room clerk to appear.

Salter guessed that this was the first chance he had had to talk all day.

'I'm from Toronto,' Salter agreed.

'That's what I figured. And you ain't on vacation, either, or you'd not be wearing a tie. You're in some kind of business, I reckon. Selling?'

Salter showed his card. The garrulity dried up as the man went behind his counter to see what Salter wanted.

'Look at this picture,' Salter said.

The owner held the picture up to the light from the window, then put it back in Salter's hand. 'He ain't been in this year yet,' he said.

'You know him?'

'Used to come in twice a week during the summer last year.'

'Overnight?'

'Now I don't know how long he stayed. He used to come in the afternoon and he was gone the next morning. It's none of my business how long people stay. He was a pretty good customer.'

'Nobody's ever going to quote you, but I'd like to know. How long did he stay?'

'Couple of hours.'

'Was he on his own?'

'He didn't come here to rest. He always had a person with him.'

'What kind of person?'

'A woman.'

'Would you know her if I showed you a picture?'

'Wasn't always the same one. The one I noticed particularly used to wear a big babushka and them dark glasses that go round, and she always stayed in the car while he registered. Then she would scamper to the room.'

'What was his name?'

'He signed in as Henry Irving, but I was no more fooled by that than I would have been if he'd signed as Spencer Tracy. I got his car licence number. If you check it you'll find he's called Alec.' He thumbed through a box of registration cards and pulled one out. 'There.'

Salter wrote down the licence number, though the identification was already certain. 'Alec?'

'That's what I heard her say one time. I was cleaning the room next to theirs. I tried to make a bit of a noise to let them know I was there, but they didn't seem to mind. I didn't hear him call her anything. Maybe he didn't know her name.'

'And you got no idea of what she looked like?'

'I never caught a proper glimpse all the times they came. As I say, I don't think it was the same one every time. Know what I mean?'

'I think I follow that. OK.' Salter turned away from the counter.

'I thought you might be in need of a room.' The clerk nodded through the window at Salter's car.

'It's a bit early in the day for me.'

'She in the police, too?'

'I'm taking her back to Toronto.'

'What's she done?'

'I don't know yet.'

As Salter opened the door, the clerk said, 'One time, somebody followed him.'

Salter came back and closed the door.

'After they was inside, a car came up the driveway. I got ready to check them in, and it went right around the office and stopped.' He moved his finger in an arc, tracing the path of the car past the office. 'Stopped, backed up and took off. There was only one thing they could be doing. Checking to find the car.'

'You're very observant, you know that? Did you see who it was?'

'A fella. That's all. In a little grey compact. That's all I remember.'

WHEN HE GOT OUTSIDE he saw to his surprise that Julie was out of the car and seemed to be waiting. When he reached her, she said, 'Which room?'

It took more than a moment, but when he realized what she was saying, all he could do was repeat the question. 'Which room?'

Then she turned, got back into the car, and stared out the window on her side. When he got in beside her, she said, 'You were working?'

'Yeah. I was trying to trace someone.'

She was very angry and for most of the drive home she refused even to look in his direction. But he had to know, and passing the Exhibition grounds, he said, 'You thought I was getting a room for us?'

She leaned back and looked at him, still saying nothing.

'And you were going to say yes?' he added, stumbling on.

'I would've said yes thirty-four years ago, but you were too chicken to ask.'

Now it was Salter's turn to be silent.

She had had an hour to compose her remarks. 'You never committed yourself, never exposed yourself, like I just did, then. I'd made up my mind, but you never risked it. You could have had me thirty-four years ago, and you could have had me back there today. Nothing changes, does it?'

Salter, too, had had a chance to reflect. 'I don't believe it,' he said. 'Maybe now. Not then. You never gave me any sign. Not then.'

'I didn't know any signs. You were the one with the signs, or so you acted. The one with all the experience.'

'That came later.'

'Were you a virgin then?'

'Nearly.'

'Oh boy. What about me? What was I to you?'

'I don't think I ever got that straight. I couldn't imagine marrying you and I couldn't imagine you would settle for anything else. I didn't know about girls like you. My mother cleaned houses during the Depression. Your mother's, probably.'

She laughed, a short, manufactured laugh. 'When you asked me to go to the races, I wondered. Then when you turned into that motel, I thought, finally, after all these years we're going to finish something we started in nineteen fifty-seven. I used to wonder then what it would be like in general, and a few times since then I've wondered what it would be like with you. Just curiosity, it's come down to, not lust. Now I know.'

'What do you mean?'

'I mean I've just found out what happens when you go to a motel with Charlie Salter.'

'What?'

'Nothing. Not then. Not now. I was feeling just as shy and nervous as I would have back then. If you'd realized what I was thinking—in time, I mean—what would you have done?'

'I'd have been very, very nervous.'

'Still? Of me?'

'Just as I would have back then.'

And then she laughed. 'What a responsibility you would have had. You wouldn't have, but you think you would. Nothing's changed. Drop me at the corner of Bay and Gerrard. I want to pick up some shampoo.'

As she got out of the car, he said, 'If I come to Ottawa, should I look you up?'

'Of course. I'd like you to meet my husband. I've often talked about you.'

'You mean I've missed my chance?'

'Of course you've missed your chance.' Then she smiled, relenting slightly. 'You could try me again in thirty years.'

FOURTEEN

'NO ONE KNEW HIM around Fort Erie,' Salter said to Peterman the next day. 'He wasn't betting. He was spending his afternoons in a motel room.'

'Who with?'

'Not Connie Spurling. She checked up on him.' He told Peterman how Joe Euringer had satisfied Spurling that Hunter was an habitué of the racetrack. 'Penny Wicklow, you know, Granny in the play, was in the same company last year. She might know.'

'I know. She might not tell you, though.'

'Why?'

'Might've been her. She's not exactly past it. How you going to handle it?'

'One of the women in the company last summer committed suicide. I thought I'd ask her about that, then ease into the other.'

Peterman looked at his watch. 'It's only nine. Do actors get up that early?'

'Let's find out.'

Without calling ahead he pressed the buzzer of Penny Wicklow's flat on Madison Avenue. Wicklow opened the door and stared at Salter with a 'what-are-you-selling?' stance. She looked, or acted, like someone who had been disturbed: shiny from a shower and wearing door-answering clothes—last night's formal sweater over a pair of paint-stained blue jeans. When she recognized him she made some hair-smoothing gestures and pulled her jeans into alignment.

Salter waited for her to ask him in, but she continued to look as if she did not want him to see the pile of dirty laundry in the middle of the living-room, hesitating long enough for him to say, 'It won't take long.'

She stepped back then and preceded him up the stairs. In the living-room she again hesitated before inviting him to sit down, perching herself on the edge of a chair. The room was more or less exactly as Salter had expected, littered and hung about, rather than furnished and decorated. The walls were covered with objects and printed matter, and there was an assortment of things to sit on, including a milking stool and a property throne made of plywood and painted gold.

'We've been looking into Hunter's past,' Salter said. 'Trying to find anything to lead us to what he was doing getting killed in a lakeshore motel.'

'He went to pay off a bookie,' Wicklow said promptly, in a voice to cut off argument.

'Did he tell you that?'

'Everyone knows. Connie Spurling gave him the money.'

'That's what we are trying to establish. He used to gamble when he was playing in Brighton last summer, didn't he?'

She looked at him, spending enough time before replying so that Salter knew she was going to answer carefully. 'So he used to say.'

'He used to go to Fort Erie a couple of times a week, I've heard.'

'That's what he said.'

Salter had picked up enough from her watchfulness to leave the topic, to return to it later. 'I came across another incident that I wondered about. I doubt if it has anything to do with the case, but it might.'

'Mary Mikhail.'

'You found her, I believe.'

'Me and Sonia Lewis. She hadn't appeared for an appointment to refit our costumes, so we went over to the house and there she was.'

'Quite a shock.'

'We were horrified. I've never known a suicide before.'

'You realized right away what had happened?'

'She took an overdose of secobarb.'

'Any idea why she did it?'

'She was depressed.'

'What about? Anything particular, or just generally sick?'

'It was about me.' Johnny Matera, the hero's brother in the play, appeared in the doorway of the bedroom dressed in chinos and a cotton sweater, smelling strongly of deodorant. He came in and sat down. 'Let's cut a long story short,' he said. 'When she first went down to Brighton, Mary Mikhail was my girlfriend. I drove down a few times to be with her, but I was working as a waiter at the time, looking for another acting job, and I didn't have time to run down there every day. Then a couple of times she was too busy to see me for long, and another once or twice she wasn't there at all, taken off for a drive or something even though she knew I might turn up. Then I met Penny, and pretty soon I was driving down to see her, instead. Mary found out; Mary and I were pretty well washed up already, so she said fine. But she cared all right, enough to off herself.'

'I think she was depressed about a lot of stuff,' Wicklow said, apparently in an effort to dilute the effect that Matera was having. She seemed to Salter an intelligent woman.

'So there you are,' Wicklow concluded. 'Nothing to do with Alec Hunter. I don't think I ever saw them together.'

Matera rubbed his sweater slowly up and down his chest, using it like a piece of sandpaper to buff his torso. 'It's got nothing to do with Hunter,' he confirmed.

'Anything strange around Hunter has got to be checked on,' Salter said.

'That's what I mean. This wasn't around Hunter.'

'Fine,' Salter said. 'Now leave me alone for a minute, would you?'

Matera looked as if he might refuse this one, but a quick placatory gesture from Wicklow got him on his feet. 'I was on my way,' he said. 'I have to work out. I'll be back with the lunch.'

'HE LIVES HERE,' Wicklow said, when she had finished smiling at the closing door. 'With me.'

'Tell me about Hunter while you were at Brighton. Was he as well-liked there as he was in your play at the Estragon?'

'We worked together, and off-stage I kept my distance. That was easy enough with Connie Spurling around.'

'I keep hearing that. Was she there all the time?'

'Most nights. She had to drive up to Toronto every morning and come back at the end of the day. She was always there when the curtain came down.'

'And in the afternoons he was at the races.'

'So I believe.'

'Did he win much?'

'As I told you, I kept my distance, but towards the end of the summer he always seemed to be broke or worse.'

'Did he always go by himself?'

'I think so. Apart from Connie Spurling, he went everywhere by himself.'

'Did you see anyone else hanging around the theatre, waiting for Hunter?'

'Like who?'

'You know how Hunter got killed. Like thugs.'

'This is *Kiss Me Kate*? No, I never saw anyone around like that.'

'Do you remember if Hunter ever went to Buffalo?'

'No, I don't. Look, I wish I could be more help but don't forget I was having my own problems keeping quiet my relationship with John. Even after Mary died, we kept it quiet for as long as we could. I didn't want to be the woman who caused it all. But it wasn't like that. As John said, he and Mary were in trouble before I came along. First they were in trouble, then he met me, but that isn't the way it would have looked.'

And that was all. But it was something.

BACK AT THE OFFICE he learned he was wanted by the deputy.

'I'm calling Horvarth in for a chat,' Mackenzie said. He looked at his watch. 'Eleven o'clock. He wants you here.'

'Why me?'

'He seems to think you're on his side.'

'If I have to bet, I am. I told you, he's angry, but I don't think he's worried about his neck. Who else will be here?'

'It's going to be quite a party. The Mountie who took the pictures, and his boss—the Mountie wants a witness, too—you and me.'

'But it isn't a formal inquiry.'

'I told you. A chat. But if word of it gets out when we go to the formal stage, I could be in trouble. I've half a mind to scrap it, hand it over to Internal Affairs, give Horvarth his hour. You know why I don't?'

Salter let him have his little drama. 'No. Why?'

'Because I'm taking your word for it about Horvarth, that he's got answers, and I'm remembering that *my* boss is an old hand, too, and he might ask me why I didn't have a little chat before the newspapers printed a story about one of our people being hauled up for an inquiry about being on the take, and then the second story about how he was cleared which everyone will assume was some kind of cover-up. See?'

AT ELEVEN O'CLOCK the group was assembled, waiting for Horvarth, who was known to be in the building, but who had not made his appearance in the deputy's office. The two Mounties sat apart, the young one, no more than twenty-two or three, sitting upright in his chair, avoiding all eyes, nervous, but with a face set with self-justification. His partner, an older man, sat pointed slightly away from his colleague, waiting for them to get on with it.

'Constable Hicklin and Sergeant Derry,' the deputy said. 'Staff Inspector Salter. Sergeant Horvarth requested his presence,' he added as the two Mounties looked at Salter. 'And here's Horvarth.'

The sergeant came through the door, looked at Hicklin, nodded at what he saw, and sat down. There was still the suggestion of the host of children's parties around his bright cheeks and blue eyes, but primarily Horvarth looked content.

'Right,' the deputy said, moving some papers unnecessarily around his desk. 'This is just a little get-together, off the record, see where we go from here. Right, Sergeant Derry?'

Derry nodded. 'We might leave early,' he said.

'I understand that. Now where shall we start?' He looked at Horvarth.

Horvarth shrugged, wonderingly.

The deputy looked at the constable. 'You took these pictures?'

The Mountie's face seemed to inflate slightly, his mouth set in a defensive, but righteous, near-pout. He looked to his sergeant for guidance.

'He took them,' Derry said.

Horvarth said, 'I understand there were two incidents. What was the first?'

The deputy looked at Constable Hicklin, who, getting the nod from his sergeant, said, 'The first incident took place at Greenwood.'

'When?'

The constable said, 'April twelfth.'

Horvarth looked curious and took a diary from his pocket. He thumbed through the pages, nodded and made a visible effort at remembering.

Salter, knowing that Horvarth had already checked this, and knowing now that Horvarth knew exactly what he was doing, thought: Don't milk it. Get your pound of flesh, but not ounce by ounce.

'That's right. I was there.'

They waited for the Mountie to continue.

'I observed you taking money from one of the bettors,' Hicklin said.

'That's right,' Horvarth agreed, remembering. 'You and I were together that day. I was showing you around, pointing out the players.'

'You went off to make a bet, and I observed you collecting money from one of the bettors in the area by the betting windows.'

Once more Horvarth made an effort to remember. Then, 'Could you ask Sergeant Lindstrom to come in?'

The deputy looked at Horvarth warningly and was met with a blank look. He picked up the phone and ordered Lindstrom into his office.

It took only a minute, long enough for everyone to have trouble trying not to fidget, all except Horvarth who was thumbing through his diary, and the deputy who was watching him.

Lindstrom walked through the door and immediately shook hands with Horvarth. 'How you been?' he asked. 'We miss you.'

'Sit down, Lindstrom,' the deputy said. 'Before anything more gets said, we're just having a little chat, nothing to do with you, off the record.'

Lindstrom sat down and looked warily around at the others. Horvarth smiled back at him.

'Have you two been in contact since Sergeant Horvarth went on leave?' the deputy asked.

'I got your orders, sir. We haven't spoken to each other.'

'Right.' The deputy looked at Horvarth.

'April twelfth at Greenwood,' Horvarth said. 'Remember?'

Lindstrom tried and shook his head.

'Yes, you do. Blitzkrieg Days won the third race.'

Lindstrom broke into a smile. 'Remember that, all right. I got the triactor.'

'What else happened that afternoon?'

'You were there. With him.' He nodded at the Mountie.

'I know. What happened after you collected your money?'

'That's when you saw me.'

'And what happened?'

Lindstrom made another small effort at remembering, and laughed. 'I gave you back the fifty I owed you.'

'Thanks.'

'That's all, Lindstrom,' Mackenzie said, not looking up.

Lindstrom got up, looking perplexed. 'That it?' Then he realized most of what the little chat must be about. 'See you later, Joe.'

'You want to carry on with this?' Sergeant Derry asked the constable.

'He can't deny the pictures,' Hicklin said.

The deputy held up one of the photographs of Horvarth and the bookmaker. The money was in the hands of both men.

Again, Horvarth stared at it, innocent and wondering.

You've gone too far, Salter thought, seeing the deputy understand that Horvarth was up to something, and not looking pleased.

'Would you ask Sergeant Visser in, and tell him to bring in what I gave him?' Horvarth asked.

The deputy gave the order and said, for the benefit of the Mounties, 'Sergeant Visser keeps the keys to the evidence safe.'

When Visser arrived, he handed over a brown envelope. The deputy nodded for Visser to go away, and opened the envelope as the door closed. Inside was a stack of hundred-dollar bills.

It was all Horvarth's show now. 'Take a good look at them, sir,' he said. 'Hold one up to the light.'

'I don't have to,' the deputy said, throwing the envelope away from him across the desk. 'There's a description on the envelope. They're phoney. Counterfeit. Well?'

'Those bills were handed to me by Jack Spicer, a bookmaker, the man in the picture. One of his clients had passed them on to him in settlement of a bet.

When Spicer tried to use one of them, he found out he'd been had. He called me—we get along well; I've arrested him twice—and asked me what he should do about them. He'd take the loss, or someone would, but he wanted to earn brownie points with us for being a good citizen, except where his business is concerned. So we arranged to meet and I took them off him and brought them back here and handed the package over to Sergeant Visser for safekeeping. I was going to deliver them to the fraud squad, but before I could do that I was sent on leave.'

'Let's go, son,' the Mountie sergeant said.

THE AIR WENT OUT of the room with them.

The deputy said, 'Well, Horvarth, you had your hour. Now I'm going to have mine. Why couldn't this have been cleared up right away?'

'I wanted to know who took the pictures. I was afraid it might be Lindstrom. Then, when I heard about the first incident, I had a pretty good idea, but I wanted to be sure.'

'The kid was being a bit zealous. That's still no reason for all this song and dance.'

'I taught that kid. He was in a course I gave them. Then, when he was assigned here, we worked together.'

Salter said, 'How long has he been on the gambling detail?'

'A couple of months.'

Salter said, 'He came to town, the young idealist, and caught his teacher right away, taking money. Then he caught him again. It was all obvious to him. They write plays about stuff like this.'

Horvarth said, 'All he had to do in the first place was ask who the guy was who was paying me off,' as he thought. 'Who Lindstrom was, I mean.'

The deputy said, 'It probably never occurred to him that a member of the Met's gambling squad was a gambler. OK, Horvarth, we had our little chat and it never happened. So I did the right thing. I don't see why I should have spent such a rough week, though. We could have found out who it was some other way. You could have told me on day one what was going on. You won't do it again.'

'Of course not.'

'I'm not asking you. I'm telling you. You won't do it again. I'm shifting you to the Community Relations unit. Go and be nice to the ethnics.'

'Not back on the squad?'

'You'd be useless, don't you see? I could never trust you again.'

FIFTEEN

OUTSIDE, Horvarth said to Salter, 'That it? Am I finished?'

'For the moment, I would say so. He's not pleased with you. You made him take a chance and he didn't like that, even though it worked out.'

'You know him well, sir? Is he the type of guy who would hold a grudge?'

'I don't think so. But he doesn't have to, does he? He's transferring you.'

'Permanently? You think I'll ever get back on the squad?'

Salter understood he was being recruited. He also understood that Horvarth did belong on the gambling squad, once he'd suffered a little. Maurice Taber could be trusted on that. 'Come into my office,' he said.

'You're going to be in bigger trouble soon,' he said, when the door was closed. 'Right now he's a little shaken up and pissed off with you, but tomorrow or the next day he's going to realize what you were really up to and then he's going to look for something else to do to you.'

Horvarth now looked like every stricken clown of legend. 'What I was *really* up to?' He had not considered what would happen after he had had his satisfaction.

'You set that kid up, didn't you? Those pictures with the bookie were a little too good to be an accident. You took the money in slow motion. Why?'

Horvarth tried to speak three times, each time searching for the words to go with the look of protest. But they never came and he gave up and nodded. 'All right. I saw the look on his face when Lindstrom paid me back at Greenwood. You're wrong. It wasn't the look of an idealist who'd found out his teacher was a crook. It was the look of an ambitious cop who saw the chance to do himself some good by turning me in. He thought catching me on the take justified him, but his real motive was to do himself some good. So he never asked me about the money, and after that he watched me, and I watched him. Sure, I made certain he saw me acting suspiciously that morning, and that he had his camera with him. But I *taught* that kid. I was still supposed to be teaching him. There's other ways he could have kept his integrity.'

'Then I guess *you* are the idealist. But Mackenzie's not stupid. He'll put it all together without any help from me. And that Mountie sergeant knew what you were up to, and he'll have a bone to pick with Mackenzie. Then Mackenzie'll wonder whether you might have gone all the way to a trial just to put on your little show. You're a bit of an asshole, you know that?'

'But I had to go that far, or the Mounties would have thought he was covering for me.'

'I doubt that.'

'No one could prove I set it all up, could they?'

'They don't have to. Mackenzie just has to know it. And what about the bookie? Can you trust him to keep his mouth shut?'

'Oh, sure. What about you?'

'What about me?'

'You gonna tell him what you think? He might not get there by himself.'

'It's nothing to do with me. I'm not in his confidence. Just so long as he doesn't think I'm in yours. What did you want me there for, anyway?'

'I don't know. I just thought . . .'

'You wanted an audience. To clap, right?'

Horvarth looked at his shoes. 'Will you speak for me with him?'

'You want me to go to bat for you?'

'Yeah.'

Salter understood that this was one of those situations where if they ask you, you have to say yes. Horvarth's appeal was naked. 'I probably won't have a chance to put my oar in, but if I do, I'll tell him I don't think you're clever enough to have thought of it, or stupid enough to go ahead if you did think of it.'

'That should do it. I'd still like to get back on the squad, though.'

'Christ, Horvarth, you're asking a lot.'

Horvarth widened his eyes and crossed his legs, and Salter got a quick illusory flash of two giant feet waving in the air. 'I'm good at it,' Horvarth said.

'So the bookie said. If I get a chance, which I won't, I'll tell the deputy what Taber said. By that time you'll probably be a filing clerk in the Bail and Parole unit.'

'I appreciate it.' Horvarth stayed in his chair, silent, trying to add some silent weight to his appreciation. 'How's your own case going?'

Salter told him, 'I'm still looking for the guy Hunter bet with. I'm looking for anyone Hunter ever bet with, or anyone who knows who he bet with. I've got a guy killed because of his gambling, but I can't find out who he bet with.'

Horvarth looked at his watch, and scrambled to his feet. 'I'll take the rest of the day and tonight. You got a picture?'

Salter passed Hunter's photograph across the desk. 'Shall I get some copies?'

'This one's enough. I'll take it around. Give me your home number. I'll call you tonight.'

HORVARTH CALLED at eleven-thirty. 'I've contacted every known bookie in Toronto,' he said. 'And about fifty of the drops. I've talked to the security police at Woodbine and at Greenwood. I haven't had a smell of Hunter. No one knows him or has ever seen him. I'm prepared to guarantee that he never bet in this town.' He put a hard edge on his voice, to make his news sound as positive as the discovery of Hunter's bookie would have been.

'Then I'll start really looking somewhere else. Thanks.'

'One thing, a lot of people have seen his picture.'

'In the paper?'

'Not in the paper, no. Someone's been round before me, also looking for Hunter.'

'Who?'

'This guy mixed up with the mob?'

'Apparently not. I think they are doing the check-ing. OK, thanks.' Salter hung up and went to bed.

THERE WAS A MESSAGE for him to call Ranovic. He had the same answer. 'Derek says this gambling thing is bullshit.' Derek was the make-up man whose truck Ranovic had driven on his previous undercover as-signment. 'He says he's known Hunter for two years through his television work, and if Hunter was a gambler he kept it in the closet. But why would he do that before Connie Spurling came around? The thing is, Derek likes to bet a little and he says one gambler can always spot another.'

'It's the message I'm hearing all over. How's life at home?'

'The latest is we're going to a marriage counsellor. Linda's going to write out her point of view, why she doesn't want to get married, why she wants a baby, the whole thing. I'm going to do the same. Then the mar-riage counsellor goes over the two statements to see if there's any way we can work it out.'

'Good luck.'

THERE WAS A NEW GIRL behind the typewriter in Con-nie Spurling's office. It seemed to Salter as he intro-duced himself that she was already slightly red about the eyes, but Spurling cut in before he could intro-duce himself. Following her into her office, he came to the point immediately. 'We're looking for some other reason why Alec Hunter was killed,' he said. 'Our information was that it wasn't a gambling debt.'

'Where are you looking?'

'The usual places. He doesn't seem to have any family around, so we're looking for enemies, jealous husbands, anyone like that.'

'He had no family. A father in Vancouver, a sister in Los Angeles. He wasn't in touch with them.'

Salter waited.

'You're wrong,' she burst out. 'He was killed because he couldn't pay. He went to meet whoever it was without the money to pay him. He told me that he would be killed if he didn't pay up.'

'That day?'

'Every time. Not that day specifically, though he did remind me. But I was sick of it. I'd warned him that I couldn't, wouldn't, keep shelling out, that I wouldn't be responsible. And I'm not. Why me? Why did I have to take it? I paid enough.'

'So you didn't give him the money.'

'No.'

'None at all?'

'No. I knew I said I did, but what do you want me to do? Say "He asked me for a thousand and he said he'd be killed if he didn't pay, but I refused so he was killed"? Nice little story, isn't it? And who's to know how often I said yes? I couldn't see that it would make any difference if you didn't know, as long as you caught the killer, but if you're going to go around looking for someone he was feuding with because you don't believe in his gambling debt, you won't find anyone, and the story, with me in it, will be the chief topic of conversation backstage for months. I can just hear it, "Did you know the cops think Hunter was

killed by someone in the theatre? If you ask me, Connie Spurling caught him screwing around and paid
someone to do it. I bet she knew where he was going
that night.'' So I told you I gave him a thousand. I
didn't. I saw him off to be killed.'

'Did you tell anyone else that you gave him money?'

'Of course not.'

'Have you talked to the cast of the play since his
death?'

'I haven't been near the theatre.'

'Then they aren't going to have much to speculate
with, are they? You don't have to blame yourself; you
would have run out of money sometime, so it was just
a matter of when. All right, so he didn't have the
money to pay a debt. That changes things, sure. I was
always a little puzzled as to why someone should kill
him if he paid up. Guys like the kind we assumed he
was dealing with will usually take something on account. A thousand would hold them off for a week.
But they wouldn't want it around that they'd done
nothing about a non-payment so your story makes
more sense now.'

'So find the killer and shut up the gossip.'

'While I'm here, I'll get rid of a few questions. Let's
start with what I heard about the plans for the play.'

'What plans?'

To Salter it sounded like a genuine response, the response of a shark to the smell of meat. He said, 'The
plans to take it to Chicago.'

She nodded, losing interest. 'That was our next
stop.'

'Yours and Hunter's?'

'That's right.'

'Perry Adler seemed to have had a different idea.'

'He would have come around.' There was a gleam from her now, not a smile, but the flash of teeth as she turned for the kill.

'You were working on that, were you, when Adler came in last week?'

She looked at him, adding up the information and arriving at the crying girl, giving herself away by glancing towards the outer office. Salter reminded himself to call the girl, to tell her to say that she had been told to keep any questioning to herself.

'I had the Chicago people convinced that without Alec the play wouldn't work. Adler was threatening to yank the play, but he wanted the booking so badly he would never have gone that far. I knew that. In twenty years he's written eleven shitty plays and finally he's got a half-decent one. He wouldn't have yanked it.' Now there was a real smile, two rows of sharp white teeth.

'All right, Miss Spurling. About the thousand. I know you've spoken to no one, but we know about it now and there's a reporter who seems to have a wire into our headquarters, so if you're asked, don't confirm or deny it. No comment, and hang up. That'll be read as "yes", and everyone will still think it was gamblers, so just in case it wasn't, whoever it was might relax. See what I mean?'

'Of course. You're wrong, but that's not my concern. I'll look a lot better this way.'

SALTER TOLD PETERMAN what he had learned from
Horvarth, Ranovic and Spurling.

Peterman said, 'You think it could have been Adler? Killing Hunter to stop Spurling taking over his
fucking play?'

'It doesn't make a lot of sense. What did Hunter
need the money for if he wasn't paying someone off?
And who is this guy with an ice-cream accent and a
gold tooth? It looks like a set-up.' Like Horvarth's, he
thought. He let the idea fill Peterman's head.

'An actor?' Peterman asked. 'Which one? And
why?'

'Sex, money, or revenge,' Salter said. 'I think it's
time to check a few alibis. And I'm going to take a run
down to Brighton. Make sure there's no reason I
should have found down there for an actor to kill
Hunter.'

'I still don't see why all the dressing up.'

'It's a thing actors do. It's why they become actors.
It's the first thing that would occur to an actor. How
do you get away with murder? Dress up as someone
else, in this case, a member of the mob. Let's try a little identification parade. I want you to take that kid
from the motel to see the play, see if any of the actors
look familiar. Tell him to imagine them all with a gold
tooth and sunglasses.'

'You mean I have to see that play again?'

'You missed most of it last time. It'll be an experience.'

'Jesus. The whole play?'

'Unless he makes an ID in the first five minutes.'

SALTER DECIDED he just had time to catch another important theatrical engagement. *The Monkey's Paw* was opening for three lunch-hour shows in the basement of an office building on Adelaide.

Salter made it in time for the opening. He sat at the back to avoid embarrassment, but it was a tiny theatre and he was extremely uncomfortable for the first five minutes as he watched from about ten feet away his son hammering away in a travesty of a cockney accent. The audience seemed eager to be pleased, though, and Seth died, offstage, fairly early, so Salter was able to watch the rest of the melodrama without discomfort and join in the enthusiastic applause at the end. He went backstage by clinging on to the dais and finding a gap in the backdrop and found Seth being embraced by his stage mother who was at least fifteen years younger than her rôle and managing the part as successfully as Wicklow managed the rôle of Granny.

Seth broke away when he saw his father. 'What did you think, Dad?'

Salter had been around show business long enough now to know the form. 'Wonderful,' he said, hugging Seth and shaking hands with everybody in sight. 'Terrific,' he said to the director. 'Fabulous,' he said to the girl taking tickets on his way out.

That night, on the phone to Annie, he said, 'Embarrassing, but I think he's probably a better actor than he was a dancer.'

SIXTEEN

THE FOLLOWING MORNING Peterman caught him in the office before he left for Brighton.

'I was thinking,' Peterman said. 'The sash-cord.'

Salter waited to see what Peterman was talking about.

'The sash-cord,' Peterman repeated. 'You know, the ligature the guy used to strangle Hunter. Where did he get it?'

'What does it matter?'

'It's the only bit of evidence the killer left behind. What we're saying now is that someone garrotted him to look like the mob did it. Why sash-cord? Because it's thin, unbreakable, and easy to buy. Buy it's also not that common. You can buy it at the hardware store, but I've been looking around. How many sash windows are left on your street?'

'Most of us have the new storms and screens now. I changed over about two years ago. I got sick of lugging the storm windows up from the basement.'

'So did most other people. Now, how many hardware stores are there in Toronto? Lots, right? But take the area between the Spadina and Avenue Road, north of Bloor all the way up to St. Clair. How many in that area? Can you name two? I've been looking at the addresses of the actors. All but two live in the Annexe, all the ones who could have been the guy with the gold tooth. So I thought I'd do a small survey. When would you think a guy planning to do a little garrotting on a Sunday would buy a piece of sash-cord? On the Saturday, right? That's what I figure. I'm going to ask around, see if I can find someone who bought about four feet of sash-cord on Saturday.'

'You think the stores will remember?'

'Maybe he used a credit card. You could be a good actor and still not too sharp, wouldn't you think?'

'Lotsa luck. I'll see you when I come back from Brighton.'

Privately, he thought Peterman's sash-cord idea absurd, and he doubted that Peterman himself was serious, but chasing down to Brighton again might be just as futile.

'HOW'S THE CAR?'

Sergeant Brock looked up, startled. Finding no one at the desk, Salter had walked through to the sergeant's office. He stood in the doorway waiting to be recognized.

'Salter,' Brock said. 'From Toronto. Right. Come in. Yes, you were here when Hambone smashed into it.'

'Twice.'

'Yes. Come over here. Look out there. See that space in the corner with the barricades around it? That's mine. When I get the car back, I figure even if Hambone backs into the barricade at top speed, I'll just get scratched. Now what can I do for you? The case of the garrotted gambler. Right?'

'What's that guy putting in grade stakes for?' Salter pointed to a construction worker hammering wooden pegs into the ground at intervals.

'Oh, that? I'm getting them to resurface it. Look at it. It's a disgrace, full of potholes.'

'New gravel?'

'Asphalt.' Brock looked at him blandly.

Salter sat down. 'Can I have a look at the story of the woman who committed suicide last summer? The costume designer?'

'What was her name again?'

'Mary Mikhail.'

Brock typed the name into his computer. 'What do you want to know?'

'Everything.'

The sergeant switched off the machine and opened a filing cabinet, pulling out a thin red folder. 'There's copies of it in here.'

Salter took the file and looked around for a space to spread it open.

'Take my desk. I have to speak to that guy out there.'

Salter read it through, starting with the hospital account. Mary Mikhail had arrived at the emergency room without any vital signs. Attempts to resuscitate her had failed. The autopsy revealed nothing except the massive dose of secobarb she had taken, the obvious cause. Salter waited for Brock to return and asked for directions to the house where Mikhail was living.

'You found something fishy about the death?'

'Not as far as you're concerned. She took a big dose of secobarb all right. I'm interested in the why's.'

'She was depressed. Says so, here. They all testified.'

'There might be a reason, though. Thanks. Can I borrow this for a while?' He held up the file. 'Glad you got the car sorted out. And the new gravel will look nice.'

'Asphalt. Very expensive. You've no idea how much asphalt it takes to fix that lot.'

THE HOUSE WHERE Mary Mikhail died was made from the local stone at the end of the nineteenth century. It was set in the middle of a big lot, two blocks from downtown. There was a sign outside, VISITORS AC-COMMODATION.

The door stood open, and as Salter was wondering whether to shout or knock, a voice behind him said, 'Inspector Salter of the Toronto Police.'

She looked about forty-five, thin, dark, wearing blue jeans and a white cotton T-shirt. She was carrying a trowel. 'I'm Carole Verdun. Come around the back. I'll talk to you while I'm finishing weeding this bed.'

Salter looked around and realized he was in the presence of a gardener. There were flowers everywhere, big ones against the house, beds of small ones in front and around the silver birch in the middle of the lawn, and everywhere the soil had a light, freshly turned look.

Behind the house there was a flagstone patio, more flowers and what looked like a vegetable garden at the end. She led him to one of the garden chairs, and moved away to a nearby bed where she was putting in a row of border plants.

'I'll make you some tea in a minute, as soon as I've finished this.' She knelt down and began to rummage in the soil.

'That looks very friable,' Salter said.

'What?'

'The soil. Friable. I've read the word a hundred times but this is the first chance I've had to say it.'

'Is that good?'

'I think so. It always sounds like it.'

'Friable,' she repeated, then got back to work.

'How did you know who I was?'

'The whole town knows who you are. I've had two phone calls about you. I half-expected you. There.' She stood up and scratched her belly, leaving a large smudge. 'Now I'll make us some tea.'

'Not me.'

'Well, *I'm* having tea and you can wait and watch.' She seemed to be speaking to an old friend who she knew wouldn't take offence. 'Do you garden?'

'I cut the grass.'

'I was going to suggest you walk around and admire my planting, but you'll just have to sit there until I'm ready.'

She went inside, and returned before long with a mug of tea and sat down across the garden table. 'What do you want to know?'

'Mary Mikhail,' Salter said.

She nodded slightly over her tea.

'Why did she commit suicide?' Salter asked.

'The coroner said . . .'

'I know what the coroner said. What do you think?' Salter had decided to trust this woman with the New York accent, responding to the way in which she seemed at home in the world, unruffled by the appearance of policemen on her lawn.

She nodded. 'I've had plenty of time since then and we've put together a lot of sightings.' She sipped her tea and took a cigarette from a pack on the table. Two of her fingers were stained a dark orange. 'She used to go for drives during the afternoon. In the natural course of things in the country, people saw her and told each other they saw her. The primary field for gossip around here is about six miles, though you can pick up vibes beyond that. Her picture was in the local paper when she died. Putting it all together, I've come to the not very startling conclusion that Mary was jilted. Is that the word any more?'

'Who by?'

'Again, this is one of the things us country folks have in our bones. I know, you understand, but I don't know how I know.' As she said this, she affected to rock herself in her chair to accompany her parody of a rustic dialect.

'Who?'

'Alec Hunter.'

Salter accepted the gift and set it aside for the moment.

'Who were your tenants when she died?'

'All of them: Mary, Penny Wicklow, Sonia Lewis, and Bill Turgeon. I had them all for the summer.'

'Hunter?'

'Not him, no. He wanted to, but I told him to find somewhere more discreet.'

'You have strict rules?' He was surprised. She didn't seem the type.

'About noise, and fuss, and general upset. I don't mind who sleeps with who, but they can't do it in my house because they get into arguments at three o'clock in the morning, especially actors, meaning actresses too, and I don't need it. I came here to get away from the rat-race, for a little serenity, and that's what I intend to have.'

'Where are you from?'

'Manhattan. I had a travel agency, but I decided that the street stuff was getting to much for me—don't get me wrong: I love New York—but living there makes you old before your time, so one day I packed my bags and went looking for a place where I could grow a garden and read. And I wound up here. This was ideal, because I also like fishing, and I like to go to the theatre, and I can get to Niagara, and, with a bit of effort, to Stratford. I can also go to Toronto, but that town is so expensive I don't bother much. In the winter I go to Europe.'

'In the winter?'

'It's the best time. But enough of me, what else do you want to know?'

'Anything you can tell me about the people who stayed with you. Mary Mikhail. The report says she was manic-depressive.'

'She wasn't. They all said that because she was upset for a time, before she died. I've told you why.'

'What did she do in her spare time?'

'When she wasn't driving around the countryside? Most of the time she was working or sitting where you are, reading.'

'Was she friendly with the other people in the house?'

'They all got along. Penny Wicklow had a boy-friend, of course, that Matera character. And I believe, no, I know, that there was a connection between Mary and Johnny Matera early in the summer. More than that, Mary, I'm pretty sure, dumped him, and Penny picked him up. As for Sonia, she was a home-body. She used to help me a lot around here.'

'Bill Turgeon?'

'He came and went. He didn't often join us after the play.'

'You all got together every night afterwards?'

'Let me tell you how this house works. I like people, OK? And I can't quite afford to run this place without a bit of income. So I decided to open a bed-and-breakfast. That was all right, I had lots of business, but it kind of tied me down, and anyway they closed me up.'

'Who?'

'The town council. I was the first, then there were a couple of others opened, then the town council passed a by-law prohibiting bed-and-breakfast places in residential areas, which included all of us.'

'Why?'

'They said the neighbours objected, and that sounded possible, but the real reason is that the town council contains three councillors who own motels.'

'You've still got the sign.'

'No, I haven't. The sign says ACCOMMODATIONS. That could mean anything and their by-law specifically says "bed-and-breakfasts", so I've hired a lawyer to fight the bastards, but he says they'll just pass a by-law against signs. I don't care much, except for the principle, because in the meantime I slipped along to the theatre and let it be known that I had some bedrooms for the summer and I filled up as soon as they saw them. The only rule I have is no sex where I can see it or hear it. Sounds a little quaint in this decade? It is, but I can get away with it. To compensate, the whole house is theirs, including the living-room where we generally gather after the performance before everyone goes to bed. I cook—I'm a good cook— and they are welcome to have friends in for dinner. Not breakfast. And for the price, they get a very good deal. And so do I. After a couple of weeks, I'm just a cook and den mother with help from them if I need it, and I can even get away for a few days and leave them to get on with it. I'm fully booked for the summer season, and as soon as they arrive, I take the sign down.'

Salter said, 'Is that tea still warm? I wouldn't mind some now.'

When she returned with a mug for him, he said, 'To be honest with you, I'm not too concerned with Mary Mikhail. I'm investigating another case.'

'So I hear. Alec Hunter. That's why I told you the gossip, but I hardly knew him. I'm glad I didn't have him in the house because I didn't like him much, what I saw of him. He came around once or twice to see

Bill, but I understand he had his own apartment downtown.'

'As far as you knew then, he wasn't involved with any of your... ladies?'

'No, but then he had a permanent lady, didn't he, and I wouldn't have known anyway. My house rules would work against any hanky-panky he might want to get up to here.' She put her empty cup on the table. 'Certainly not with Sonia. She was having what she called a relationship with a boy she'd met waiting on tables in Toronto. She spent most of her time in the house in case he called. The phone bill was horrendous, but I deducted some because Sonia did a lot of work for me between calls. And the only other possibility is Penny, Penny Wicklow.' She stood up to end the topic, 'You want to see the scene of the crime?'

Salter realized that the connection between Mikhail and Hunter was public knowledge locally which he was welcome to, but he was not going to hear any unsubstantiated gossip. They went into the house which was much as Salter had expected—comfortable, cool, personal and altogether a very desirable place to stay for the summer. She led him upstairs to a wide landing leading to the bedrooms. All the doors were open, and the whole second floor was full of scents from the garden below.

'This was Mary's room.' It was a room in which a lot of time could be spent. A bed, a polished floor with several small rugs; a comfortable armchair angled so the reader could look out the window over the garden; a nearly full bookcase, a bureau with a lighted mirror above it, and a desk and chair. It looked like the guest bedroom in a private house.

'Nice,' Salter said. 'How much do you charge?'

She smiled. 'Forty a night, less by the week, but it's hard to get in.' She led him out to the landing. 'There's just one bathroom, but there's a separate john, and they can use mine if they have to. I live downstairs at the back. It isn't a problem, because every room has a decent mirror in it and they all bring their own hair-driers.'

'Were you in the house when it happened?'

'I was taking a nap in my "concierge's" quarters downstairs and I heard a heck of a row upstairs. Afterwards I realized I had heard Penny scream and then Sonia and then a lot of running across the hall and down the stairs. By the time I'd got a wrap on, Penny was on the phone and I could hear Sonia having hysterics. I went upstairs and found Bill guarding the door to Mary's room and Sonia still hysterical. Bill told me Mary was dead and to look after Sonia, which I did. The medics arrived in a couple of minutes. I think they tried to revive her but she was gone. We followed them to the hospital in my car.'

'You left Sonia Lewis here?'

'No, we all went after the ambulance. When they pronounced Mary dead, we came back and I made tea, which was all I could think of to do.'

'So, just to get it straight, the two women found her and then Bill Turgeon heard the noise and came out to help. Then Wicklow called the ambulance, then you appeared?'

'That's it. Why?'

'I don't know. Something in the police report. Just a detail. Where did the others stay? Who had which room?'

They toured the landing while she opened doors. 'This was Penny's, across the hall. This was Sonia's, and Bill had the room at the front, the furthest from the bathroom, but the best in every other way.'

The other three rooms differed in their furnishings but the level of comfort was the same.

'Did they have room keys?'

'None of the rooms lock. I put good locks on the closets and on the desk drawers. I've never had a problem, and they give each other the freedom of their rooms when they're out. Sometimes one of them will call from the theatre to ask another to pick up something they've forgotten. I explain all this in detail before they come and them as wants to bar their doors can go somewhere else. I lock the front door, though, and give them keys for that.' She walked ahead of him down the stairs.

In the hall, Salter asked, 'What did you do with her stuff?'

'After the police finished I packed it into her suitcases and put it in the basement, waiting for someone to pick it up. Her mother is an invalid living in Victoria, but her sister, who lives in England, is planning a visit and she's promised to deal with it then. It's still in the basement.'

'Can I have a look at it?'

'I guess so.'

There were two suitcases and a small square toilet case. Salter looked through the suitcases and gently stirred the contents of the toilet case with his finger.

'What are you looking for?'

'The drugs Mary Mikhail took. Where's the bottle? Do you remember one?'

'It would have been empty. I could have thrown it out.'

'Did you?'

She looked startled, then nodded slowly. 'Right. No. It's too significant, isn't it? I'd have given it to the police. No,' she repeated. 'I didn't find one.'

'Who cleaned the room?'

'I did. I usually do if I have time, then I get to keep the quarters that have rolled under the bed. I do have a woman who comes in twice a week for the light work—I hate polishing and dusting, and shining silver, but I usually do the rooms myself. In this case it seemed important because it was kind of delicate. You never know what people might be hiding—I've had some odd stuff left behind—and Mary might not have bothered to tidy up before she took the pills. But I didn't find anything, not even a love-letter. I haven't been much help, have I? I hardly knew Hunter well enough to recognize him on the street.'

SALTER LEFT THE HOUSE and drove around until he found the fire hall. Behind it, as he suspected, he found the ambulance station.

He had no trouble finding the attendant who had handled Mikhail's suicide. It had been one of the more interesting assignments of the previous summer—most of his work was responding to highway accidents—and he remembered the details clearly.

'We got a 911,' he said. 'When we arrived there was a woman waiting for us in a panic, and some guy guarding the room. The woman said they had found her just a few minutes before. The police have all the names.'

'Did you try to revive her?'

'It was a job for a stomach pump, but it was too late even for that. She was full of sleeping pills.'

'How did you know?'

'The attendant tried to remember. 'We knew all right, because I remember reporting it to the hospital so they could pump her out.' He thought his way back. 'And we didn't search for drugs, which we'd normally do. See, if you can tell them at the hospital what they've taken, they have a better chance, so we always have to look around for the cause. But I don't remember seeing anything. No, I think one of the women told us.'

'You didn't find any container? No pill bottle?'

'I don't think so. No. One of the women told us and we took her word.'

Back in his car, Salter looked over the police report again. As he had remembered, there was no mention of finding a suicide note, or of the drug container, but after questioning the three people at the scene, the interviewing officer recorded that Mary Mikhail had for some time been showing symptoms of alternately depressed and excited behaviour. In place of a suicide note, the coroner had accepted as evidence of her state of mind a will form that was on the coffee table.

Salter moved on to the drugstores. There were two in town and neither one was able to supply the name of the doctor who had prescribed the drug, because neither had filled a prescription for secobarb for Mary Mikhail the previous summer. Salter made a note to try to find the name of Mikhail's Toronto doctor.

Now he began to speculate. He returned to both drugstores and came up with the information that Hunter had had filled a prescription for Zephyr, another kind of sedative, the week before Mikhail's death. A phone call to the Toronto doctor who had authorized the prescription got the information that Hunter had been using secobarb for years, but had complained about the after-effects and the doctor had changed the prescription to Zephyr some months before. Now Salter returned to the police station. He had no authority to make his next request, but he guessed that Brock could get the information.

'You know these drugstore owners?' he asked.

'Sure.'

'It's just a detail, but could you find out for me if any of these people had bought secobarb from them last summer?'

'Wouldn't they tell you?'

'They were starting to clam up. Worried about their ethics, I guess. They'd told me a lot already.'

Brock got on the phone and made the request, using first names all round.

While they waited, Salter asked, 'Who was the coroner? You know him?'

'A little bit. He doesn't like trouble, which suits me.'

'How would he react if it looked as if another doctor had been negligent?'

'He wouldn't believe it, but he'd obey the rules. He'd be more likely to give a verdict of accidental death than suicide, to save the family feelings. In a case like this, though, it was pretty clear.'

The phone rang and Brock picked it up, listened briefly, thanked the caller and put it down. 'Wicklow,' he said. 'She had a supply of secobarb just before Mikhail died. Now you are going to stir it up, aren't you?'

'I'll call you if it's going to touch you. You did your job.'

Brock shrugged. 'Let me know what you find out anyway, will you? At least she wasn't a local.'

SALTER HAD ONE LAST CALL. Twenty minutes later he pulled in to the Pioneer Motel.

The owner remembered him clearly. 'Need a room?' he asked, and winked. 'Oh no, I see you haven't got her with you this time. Well, any time, I'll give you the special rate.'

'You remember the guy I was inquiring about?'

'Henry Irving? He stayed here seven times altogether.'

'When was the last time?'

'August fourteenth.' He chuckled. 'Thought you might be back, so I did a little detective work. Here's all his registration cards. See? Twice a week for four weeks except the last. Then nothing.'

Salter took the cards. 'I'll give you a receipt for them and send them back when I'm through.'

SEVENTEEN

PETERMAN WAS WAITING for him in the office. He listened to what Salter had to say. 'So, when Matera's girlfriend died, he was already hooked up with Wicklow, which was the end of Wicklow and Hunter?'

'Looks like it.'

'You think Matera knows that Hunter had been screwing Wicklow?'

'I don't know that he was yet. But if it's true, then I would guess Matera doesn't know. Nobody else did. I don't think she'd tell him any more than she thought he could handle.'

'Does it help?'

'It's something. You taking that kid to see the play tonight?'

'That's what I was waiting to see you about. Sure, if I have to, but I was wondering if I could put it off until tomorrow.'

'What's the difference? It'll still be the same play.'

Peterman looked confused. 'That's not it. I have something fairly important on tonight.'

'That important?' Salter waited for Peterman to explain but, nothing being forthcoming, said, 'If you're seeing a marriage counsellor, I guess the play can wait until tomorrow. It's a long shot, anyway.'

Peterman nodded, not taking the bait, and picked up the phone as Salter left.

A few minutes later, as Salter was leaving for home, Peterman appeared in the door of his office. 'That kid can't make it tomorrow, or the next day, or all next week. It has to be tonight. He's got a new job.'

'That's too bad.'

'I *can't* go tonight.'

Now Salter felt the need to communicate a newly acquired anxiety to Peterman, an anxiety caused by a sense that he had been relying too much on the assumption that this was a quarrel among thugs, and that he ought to have looked elsewhere a lot sooner. 'Can't?' he asked. 'We're chasing a murderer. Going bowling?'

'No!'

'I give up.'

'All right. I'm going dancing.'

Salter perched on a desk and waited for more.

Peterman sat down, affecting a casual air. 'Ballroom dancing. We're in the semi-finals of a competition tonight.'

'Fox-trots? Stuff like that?'

'It's the Latin-American competition. We're right through to the semi-finals.'

This was wonderful. Peterman's misery was obvious, and Salter now had no doubt of the importance of the event, and there was probably no need to panic. He could go to the play himself. But before he let Peterman off the hook he felt entitled to some entertainment. 'You wear numbers?' he asked. 'Like you see on television? Big cardboard numbers on your back? Which channel should I watch?'

'Only the finals are televised.'

'You ever make it that far?'

'The best we've done so far is third in the Viennese waltz.' Peterman wriggled in his seat. 'I don't talk about this around here. Nobody else in Homicide dances.'

'You don't know that, do you? Maybe they all keep it secret, like you.' He laughed. 'OK. My wife's away. I can go. Where were you meeting the kid?'

Now Peterman looked guilty as well as embarrassed. 'Outside the theatre. Around ten-thirty.'

'Afterwards?'

'I couldn't see the point of seeing it again.'

'I'll meet him. You'd better go home and take a few turns around the living-room.' Salter imagined Peterman's slightly short legs twinkling around the dance floor. 'Good luck. And I won't say a word.'

'Thanks.'

As Salter left he heard Peterman singing a ditty. 'Hoor-ah, hoor-ay,' Peterman sang, 'my wife's on holi-day.'

SALTER DECIDED the play was good enough to stand a second viewing, but he would wait and take Annie who was always nagging him to take her to things like this. He arrived an hour before the performance and arranged for a ticket to be left for the motel clerk, then let himself in through the unguarded door into the empty theatre. Up in the box behind the back seats, the lighting man was already setting up, and Salter, remembering they had not talked to him, decided to fill in the time by ticking him off his list.

'I'm a student in third year Ryerson,' the boy said, after Salter had introduced himself. 'I don't really know any of these people except the crew.'

'Did you ever meet Hunter?'

'No, but I saw him operate once. The famous put-down.'

'When was that?'

'The night he tried to grope Penny Wicklow.'

'I heard about that. She objected pretty loudly.'

'"Take your hand off my ass," she cried, and the spectators gasped.'

'Spectators?'

'I think it was all for their benefit. He had his back to the stage and couldn't see them. When he first began to fondle her buttocks lasciviously she just rose on her toes and pushed him away.' The boy gave a saucy grin, and Salter wondered if his vocabulary and syntax were derived from watching too much Noel Coward and if he could look forward to Seth talking like this.

The boy continued, 'When she saw the others, though, she did her little number. I think she was acting.'

'What happened exactly?'

'Penny and Hunter were right below us here. He made his move. Then Matera and some others came on stage from behind, she saw them, and shouted.'

'You see a lot from here, don't you?'

'Everything. That was the most interesting, though. Now I have to get to work. I have to run through the board.'

The sound of voices came up from the auditorium. Salter looked at his watch. There was still two hours to go.

'That'll be Bill,' the lighting man said. 'Bill Turgeon, setting up.'

Salter climbed down to the auditorium and followed the sound backstage, finding Turgeon with a list in his hand, checking props.

'Saw you talking to Gerry, in the booth,' Turgeon said. 'Found the guy who killed Alec yet?'

'Got time for a coffee?'

'No, sorry. Too much to do. We could talk now, while I'm checking this list.'

'I was looking around Brighton this afternoon,' Salter said. 'Checking your old boarding-house.'

'What for? Alec didn't stay there.'

'I know. I was curious about that girl who died.'

'Mary? Yeah, that was rotten.'

'Did you know her well?'

'Only, like, in the house.'

'You found her, didn't you?'

'Me? No, I didn't find her. Penny Wicklow found her. I was in my room and I heard this scream. I came out and there they were. I sent Penny to get an ambulance. The other one, Sonia, was no good. She was having hysterics. No, I didn't even go in the room. I just stayed by the door to make sure no one came in before the ambulance got there.'

'What did you do about the other girl?'

'She went back to her room. I told her to stay out of the way.'

'You could tell Mary Mikhail was dead, I guess.'

'I didn't go near her but I could see what had happened.'

'Did you wonder why she killed herself?'

'We all did. They say she was depressed.'

'Was there a man around that you know of?'

Turgeon considered this for a few moments. 'She *was* with Johnny Matera, but they broke up. I suppose that might have done it.'

'Anyone else?'

'Not that I know of.'

'What about Hunter?'

Turgeon nodded as if expecting the question. 'It's possible, but I don't know where he could have found the time! He went to Fort Erie every chance he got.'

'By himself?'

'That's what he told me.'

'You mean that's what he told you to tell Connie Spurling. But he's dead, and I'm not Spurling. What was he doing?'

Turgeon gave Salter a rueful look. 'You must know the answer to that already. OK. I told you I covered for him. But he did lose a lot of money gambling.'

'Who was he seeing?'

'Mary Mikhail, for one.'

'Who else?'

'I don't ... ng considered about Turgeon's ulsive Don Juan. With surprised he his preoccupation with the props

Well. Even don't go

to give himself time to think. Salter thought of a way
to jolt him into spontaneity, ridiculous under the
present circumstances, but worth a try.

'What made you two such pals?'

Turgeon smiled. 'I told you, we weren't bum buddies. I did him a couple of favours, and he did me
one.'

'What kind of favours?'

'I already told you that, too. I covered for him with
Spurling. And I lent him money.'

'What did he do for you?'

'He got me this job. It's the kind of thing where you
need an "in". I don't have any training except what I
got in Brighton, and getting that job was just an accident. I was staying at this boarding-house, looking
for a job, when the company started, and they needed
someone handy backstage, which I am. I can do anything manual. But I liked the job and I asked Mr
Hunter what I should do when the company packed
up and he got me taken on here.'

'In exchange for covering for him?'

'A little back-scratching, I guess. Yes.'

'Are you going to Chicago?'

'I'm waiting to find out. I would've, if Hunter had
n't been killed.'

'You do̶ing out with him offstage, did you?'

'Only ̶̶̶̶̶̶̶̶̶̶̶ ̶̶̶̶̶̶̶̶̶̶ did that.'

her.' Gambling.'

Salter stood up. ̶̶̶̶̶̶̶ his time? Apart from

without your protecto̶̶̶̶̶

to Chicago? What were you doing before the Brighton job?'

'I was a handyman. That's how I got the job. I did some stuff for them, little things, and they asked me to go full-time for the summer. I liked the idea, and I enjoyed being with the company. I'm going to try and stay in stage work.'

'I imagine you'll do OK. One little thing. Did anyone stay in the house when they took Mary Mikhail to the hospital?'

'Not that I can remember?'

'What about the girl with hysterics?'

'She came with us.'

'Then you all came back to the house?'

'That's right.'

'Then what? Did anyone go up to Mary's room?'

Turgeon looked thoughtful. 'It's hard to remember. I didn't, but one of the others might have done.'

Salter went off for a solitary supper after calling his answering machine. He returned to find Claud Arbour waiting for him in the foyer.

'It's a terrific play,' Arbour said. 'Thank you for the ticket. But I didn't recognize anyone in it.'

'The two brothers, or the brother-in-law?'

Arbour shook his head firmly. 'No way. None of those guys looked a bit like the Italian.'

'But one of them could have been. You just didn't recognize him.'

'No way. I am sure that he was not one of them. I watched him very carefully because he was such a crooked-type guy. You know?'

'Then I'm sorry to have wasted your time, but you didn't waste mine. That's a great help.'

'No problem. I told you, it's a terrific play.'

BEFORE HE WENT to see Wicklow, Salter tracked down Sonia Lewis, the hysterical girl. She was still in bed after a late shift at The Keg, a chain restaurant that employs a lot of out-of-work actresses. At first she could not help.

'I was in shock,' she said. 'Totally gone.'

'I understand that. But before you went into shock, what happened?'

'We went to Mary's room.'

'Who was in front?'

'Penny. We got to Mary's room and Penny turned round, sort of screaming, and pushed me away, but I had already seen Mary sprawled out, and that's when I lost it.'

'What then?'

'Nothing then. I lost it.'

'A total blank?'

'I think I remember Bill running across. Yes, Penny ran down the stairs to phone and Bill grabbed me and sort of carried me to my room where I fainted.'

'When did someone say that she had taken sleeping pills?'

'I can't remember. I was gone.'

THEY TALKED to Wicklow together. First, Salter reported to Peterman on the failure of his visit to the theatre to add much to what they knew. 'And I talked some more to Turgeon, the stage manager. Hunter's only pal. I wondered what made those two such pals, but the answer is easy—Turgeon did him favours.'

'Did you find the bookie?'

'Not yet. How'd you make out last night?'

'We won.' Peterman tried to say it casually, but he couldn't suppress a large lop-sided grin.

'What next?'

'The regional finals. In Kingston. Next month. I'll have to come out of the closet.'

'Why?'

Once more Peterman gave a smile distorted by false modesty. 'They're televising them. Somebody'll see me.'

'Will you have those big numbers on?'

Peterman sighed. 'See what I mean? I'll probably have to ask for a transfer to the Communications Unit.'

MATERA WAS AT HOME, and when Salter explained that they just had a few more questions to ask Penny Wicklow, he took up a protective stance on the arm of her chair. Salter was reinforced in his impression that apart from the area of physical strength—and even in this area Wicklow looked fit enough to hold her own—their rôles might be reversed, that Wicklow was more capable of protecting Matera than the reverse.

While the two actors were conferring on whether Matera ought to stay, Peterman managed a querying look to Salter and, getting a twitch of indifference from his boss, said, 'No reason you should go, Mr Matera. We're not interrogating anyone, just trying to get some history straight.' He smiled at them both and settled himself on the plywood throne with a notebook.

Salter took a straight-backed chair. 'We've been looking into that story of the girl who committed suicide. Mary Mikhail? Everyone says she was manic-depressive—let's just say depressed. The coroner said the balance of her mind was disturbed. What set her off, do you know? What really tipped her over? You lived in the house with her. What I'm wondering is— let's see how I can put this—at the inquest you could have been taking the line of the least said the better. After all, she did commit suicide, there's no suggestion of anything else, but I wondered if you had an idea why that you kept to yourself, especially since the season still had a few weeks to run.'

'What are you talking about?'

'You see how my mind is working. If there *was* a reason that hadn't come up—a person—you might not mention it and there might be a little bit of an agreement among you to leave it lie.'

'You think there was a conspiracy?'

'Call it a meeting of minds.'

'About what?'

'Why she did it.'

Matera made to speak, but Wicklow restrained him. 'What's on your mind, Inspector?'

'I'm wondering if she was having an affair with Hunter, and he dumped her.'

The tension eased slightly. Wicklow shook her head. 'Not that we knew of. There wouldn't have been much opportunity.'

'We found some, though. Hunter wasn't at the races on his afternoons off. Part of the time he was in a motel with a lady.'

'I wouldn't know about that.'

Matera spoke up. 'It's possible she would have kept it very private, because she'd be frightened of me finding out, of what I'd do to Hunter.' He stroked his chest. 'I don't think so, though.'

Salter nodded. 'It isn't important. There are a couple of details about the inquest that bothered me, that's all, things the coroner didn't ask. For instance, was Mary Mikhail in the habit of taking sleeping pills?'

Again she looked up at Matera. 'Why don't you go ahead, John? I'll finish here and meet you somewhere after your workout. That little Italian café on Bloor, opposite Major. All right?'

Matera stood up and pushed his T-shirt into his pants. 'OK.' He turned to Salter. 'Mary didn't take pills when I knew her.'

'Thanks.'

When the door was closed, Wicklow said, 'I don't want to be accused of being uncooperative, and lying is tricky when I've got to worry about you two *and* Johnny. I'm bound to come unstuck somewhere, so let's go back a few lines. This is between us, right?'

'So long as it doesn't have any bearing.'

'It doesn't. The girl in the motel with Hunter was me, not Mary. I don't know why she committed suicide, but if you dig around that motel long enough you'll come up with someone who looks like me so I'm saving you the trouble. I'd finished with Hunter a

couple of weeks before Mary died. Johnny was right—
by that time I was seeing him and he'd just about given
up on Mary. She didn't tell me what the state of the
relationship between her and Johnny was, and naturally I didn't ask, being in the process of taking him
away from her.'

'Did you ever know her to take pills? I think I know
why the coroner didn't push it. I had shingles once and
for a couple of days I was prescribed an opium deriv-
ative for the pain. Then my doctor cut me off, because if the prescription had been filled once more
I'd've been hooked. That happened to me in hospital
once, when I had my gall bladder out. The doctor gave
me Demerol on the first night and left instructions that
I could have a sedative after that if I needed it, but the
instructions got a little mixed up and I got a shot of
Demerol every night for a week. It was terrific, until
the doctors found out. What I'm getting at is that
some coroners might have wondered about the wis-
dom of prescribing secobarb for someone who wasn't
very stable, so they might not press that part of the
inquiry too closely in case the doctor was someone
they played bridge with.'

All this was designed to give Wicklow an opportunity to realize the value of cooperating even further,
but she stayed silent.

'You didn't see any sign of a bottle around the
room?'

'That's right, I didn't.'

Peterman said, 'How did everyone know it was
secobarb if there was no bottle around?'

'I don't know. I just assumed it, I guess. Everyone said she'd taken secobarb, and that's what they found at the autopsy, didn't they?'

'It probably doesn't matter.' Salter stood up, and Peterman slid off his throne. 'And thanks for clearing up the motel stuff. One thing, though. Did Matera ever suspect that you were still involved with Hunter?'

She shook her head. 'You heard him. He wouldn't have kept that to himself.'

'But Hunter was still coming on to you during the play.'

'What do you mean?'

'He didn't give up, did he?'

'He never gave up. He couldn't believe that I'd prefer Johnny to him. How did you know?'

'Someone saw you, in the theatre, the night when you told him loudly to lay off. They said it looked a little forced.'

She made an irritated, dismissive gesture, waving her hand back and forth. 'You're wasting your time on this one. The fact is that I had no use for him by then. Try, though, to see it the way it happened. Hunter was an old lover, and he didn't care as much as I did who knew it. Connie Spurling was the brake on him, and Johnny was my Connie Spurling, if you like. Hunter was afraid of what she would do to him if she caught him playing around, and I was afraid of what Johnny would do to him. When Hunter came on to me, before I had time to tell him quietly to get lost, I saw Johnny at the other end of the theatre, and I was afraid of what it would look like. I didn't think very clearly. Because we had once been lovers I was afraid it would show, and I was trying to think how to act so that it would be clear that we never were, so I tried to make some kind of joke of it, to get a message to him, and a different message to Johnny. Johnny *hadn't* seen us, so I needn't have panicked. If this all sounds ridiculous, I'm sorry. But it's true.' She ended quietly, then added, 'And what I'm trying to get across to you, Inspector, is that Johnny didn't notice a thing, so he didn't have to go out and kill him. He was with me when Alec was killed.'

None of this sounded invented. Wicklow's words had the force and coherence of remembered truth. Salter began to feel that he had entered a blind creek. He made one more try. 'I talked to Sonia Lewis.' He searched for an invention. 'She remembered that you all knew it was secobarb right away.'

Wicklow raised her hands to stop him. 'All right, all right. Christ!' She squeezed out a breath, hugging herself. 'The pills were mine. It never came out at the inquest and I never raised it because . . . Mary was unbalanced and it was bad enough knowing she killed herself with my pills, without telling the world. Now it sounds as if it might be more important so I'm telling you.'

'You gave them to her? Enough to kill herself?'

'I'm not that irresponsible. She got one from Hunter, and it worked. I gave her another one, just one, a couple of days later. The next day she was dead, and when I checked, all my secobarb was gone.'

'Later? You didn't realize it right away?'

'No, not until the hospital said that's what it was.'

'You knew what had happened when you saw Mikhail, though,' Salter insisted. 'Somebody said "Secobarb". Was that you?'

'I guess. Who else could it have been?'

'You were the first in the room. What did you do when you saw her?'

'Screamed, turned, crashed into Sonia behind me.'

'She never came into the room?'

'I pushed her out. Then Bill came to see what the matter was and he got Sonia away while I went downstairs to phone.'

'You found the pill bottle, though?'

'No. That's something that stuck. My pill bottle was still in my room. Mary had taken the pills, but not the bottle. No, I just saw Mary, and I must have thought, "She's taken my secobarb." When I checked, she had.'

Perhaps it wasn't a blind creek after all. 'One last detail,' Salter said. 'When you came back from the hospital, did anyone go into Mary Mikhail's room?'

'Of course not. The cops were still there. They came right after the ambulance. They sealed the room for a couple of days, but there was a policeman there from the time they took Mary away.'

EIGHTEEN

'HOW DID YOU KNOW that about Hunter groping her in the theatre?' Peterman asked in the car.

'The lighting man. I'm glad we cleared that up.'

'But Hunter *was* screwing the Mikhail girl, and she did kill herself because of him, not Matera.'

'It looks like.'

'Next time I see Matera, I'll tell him. Ruin his day. Now tell me something else. Those pills came from Wicklow, right? Then what are you worrying about the bottle for?'

'How did they know it was secobarb right away?'

'Because Wicklow found the bottle right away beside the bed, and got rid of it. After she shouted it out.'

'Why didn't she say so?'

'You heard her explanation of what happened when Hunter groped her. She's operating on a split screen, that one, trying to keep Matera in the dark, and dodging us, too.'

'Maybe.'

'Pardon me for saying it, but what the fuck has all this to do with Hunter getting strangled in a motel?'

'I don't know yet. Everything, I think. I think there's a bottle around somewhere that had secobarb in it. Not Wicklow's. I want to find it.'

'Jesus, this is getting complicated. But we're still looking for an Italian-type guy with a gold tooth, and if the kid is right it isn't Adler, or Matera or Walker, so where are you?'

'Let's just keep pushing. Let's go and talk to Connie Spurling.'

IN SPURLING'S OFFICE, Salter said, 'Did you ever have anything to do with Mary Mikhail, the woman who committed suicide at the Brighton theatre?'

'I never even met her. Alec wouldn't have needed her services after the costumes were established.'

'Did Hunter ever talk about her death to you?'

'No. Why should he?'

Salter affected to look embarrassed. Peterman, picking up his cue, looked at his feet.

'What do you two think you've found out?' she demanded. 'There was nothing going on between Alec and her, if that's what you think. Wait a minute.' She took a desk diary from a drawer and flipped through it. 'When did that woman die? August sixteenth. He was with me. We met to go over his contract for *After Paris*.'

'How long have you been giving money for the bets he lost?'

'He didn't always lose. Not at first. At the end of the summer he started to bet more, and lose, and then he started to double up and I had to bail him out, then and afterwards.'

'What was he betting on?'

'You name it. He talked about football games, and basketball games, as well as racing.'

'All with your money.'

'Mostly. And then they killed him.'

'Yes. We're still trying to understand that.'

'SO WHAT HAVE WE LEARNED?' Peterman's tone was sceptical, wondering what Salter was up to.

'We've learned what we knew from the beginning, that Hunter didn't start to lose until after Mikhail died. Now maybe we should believe Horvarth, that Hunter wasn't gambling. He was being bled.'

'Who by? Matera?'

'By whoever thought he was responsible for giving Mikhail the pills.'

'So he gave her some pills, and she took too many. He didn't kill her, did he? What does he care what everyone blames him for? They all thought he was a prick anyway. Why should he pay out money?'

Salter waited patiently.

Peterman nodded. 'Right. He cared what Spurling thought, that she shouldn't know he was screwing Mikhail.' Peterman laughed. 'So he was using her money to keep her from finding out. That's a beaut. But we've still got an ID problem. It's gotta be Matera. Matera and Wicklow together maybe. Let's go get him. Dress him up and parade him in front of the kid.'

Salter let the stew of information and misinformation bubble up in his brain. 'Why would he want to kill Hunter?'

Peterman was quick to rearrange the theory. 'It's not blackmail. It's revenge. Wicklow told him that Mikhail killed herself because of Hunter.'

'So how could he persuade Hunter to meet him at the motel?'

'Christ knows. Maybe Hunter persuaded *him*?'

Salter had been going along with Peterman to give himself a chance to think. Now he shook his head. 'You were there. Did Matera seem to be lying?'

'He's an actor. That's his trade.'

'Were you awake long enough in the theatre to see him on stage? He's not that good.'

Peterman said, 'You know, sir, this isn't the way we usually work. Right about now you and I ought to be in a room with Matera, jumping him over the same ropes again and again. Same with Wicklow.'

'It might come to that. But we're missing something.'

THAT NIGHT, sitting in his kitchen, waiting for his dinner to defrost, he tried a number of scenarios, discarded for good the idea that Hunter really was involved with gamblers, and rested on the idea that Hunter was killed in revenge by someone like Matera. It didn't work. He trusted the motel clerk's identification. Finally he came back to blackmail because if it was linked to Mikhail's death and you eliminated all the obvious people, then there was only one possibility left. The only problem was how such a person had successfully imitated a tall Italian gangster with a gold tooth. And then Peterman's remark chimed in his head, and he drank half a pint of Scotch and went to bed.

HE AVOIDED PETERMAN the next morning, not wanting the holes in his theory to appear too quickly. First he called the motel clerk and arranged for him to watch a movie. Then he called Horvarth and asked him to put a name in the pipeline. Then he looked over the early statements and realized he would have to solve a problem of timing.

He had no trouble borrowing a copy of the movie he had been advising on the previous summer and arranging for it to be shown in the tiny auditorium they used for lectures. 'Don't ask questions,' Salter told Arbour. 'This is an identification parade, but you've got a few hundred faces to watch. Tell me when you see someone you recognize.'

Half the picture had gone by when the clerk shot up in his seat. 'That's him.'

'Hold it!' Salter shouted. Then, to the clerk, he said, 'Are you sure?'

'Certain. See that tricky way he drags one foot around when he runs. Anyway, he's wearing the same raincoat. That's him.'

'OK, thanks.' Salter stood up.

'Don't I get to see how it comes out?'

'You want to watch the rest of it?'

'Sure. It's pretty good.'

Salter patted the boy's shoulder. 'I'll leave you to it. I know what happens.'

Still dodging Peterman, Salter left the building and drove along Bay Street, turning into the Annexe, and stopped at St Bartholomew's House, guessing now why Hunter, on his way to argue with a thug about money, had taken the time to visit his great-aunt. The

man with the gold tooth had checked into the motel at
eight o'clock, when Hunter was visiting his great-aunt.

The night nurse was already on duty and he asked
her once more to go over her memory of Hunter's last
visit.

'I saw him come but I didn't see him go, which
means he must have stayed until after nine-thirty and
got someone else to press the buzzer for him,' she said.

'Can I go up and see his great-aunt again?'

'She's a little confused today.'

'I won't bother her if I seem to be upsetting her.'

'You know the room. Three-one-eight. Third floor.
There's the elevator, or the stairs would probably be
quicker.'

Salter took the stairs. On each floor there was an
exit sign above an outside door with a crash bar. On
the third floor Salter pushed the door open and found
a fire escape outside. He let the door close, but it was
prevented from shutting completely by a wedge in the
bottom of the frame. Salter walked to the metal plat-
form at the top of the fire escape and let the door go
again. The door stayed open just enough to let him get
his fingers along the edge and pull it open. The wedge
holding the door open was a small piece of closely-
woven cord, crushed flat but still with enough bulk to
do the job. Peterman would be pleased. Checking the
hardware stores might have paid off eventually.

Then he called Inspector Corelli and told him to
leave a message somewhere that the man who had
been playing the Mafia hit man was dead.

'IT WAS HUNTER,' Peterman said wonderingly. They had studied the autopsy again. It was all there. The traces of make-up which had been dismissed as having been left over from the performance the day before and the little cuts inside his mouth made by the dental piece he was wearing, the fake gold tooth which had cut him when he had been struck in the mouth. There was even the Swiss army knife on his key chain, the smallest version but big enough to cut sash-cord.

'So the killer could have been any shape?' Peterman said.

'Or sex. Hunter went down to that motel in disguise to kill someone. We were supposed to find someone garrotted in that motel, and we were supposed to be looking at the mob to find out his killer. And we were also supposed to find out that the killer registered at eight o'clock at the motel, and waited for his victim, while Hunter was with his great-aunt until at least nine-thirty.'

Peterman thought his way through this. 'But whoever it was had to have realized what Hunter was planning, *and* seen how he could turn it on its head. Have we met anybody that clever? Kind of rules out Matera, doesn't it?'

'He didn't have to plan it, or figure it out all at once. All he had to do was kill Hunter while Hunter was trying to kill him in that motel room, then he'd have time to think. The rest of it could occur to anybody. He had to strip Hunter of his glasses, mirror, gold tooth, cap, what else?'

'Wig, probably. Hunter was fair-haired. Remember the guy with the blond wig in the play? The clerk would have noticed a coiffure like that.'

'And gloves. Hunter would have been careful. There was quite a bundle of stuff. What did he do with it?'

'Dumped it in someone's garbage?' Peterman offered.

'I wouldn't think so. If he stripped Hunter in the first place it's because he wanted us to think, as Hunter did, that the mob had killed someone. But if we find a whole make-up kit and costume in someone's garbage, then we would forget about the mob and start looking for an actor. There's probably plenty of forensic stuff on the disguise to link it to Hunter, which, if the killer is smart, and he seems to be, he would also not want disclosed. So I don't think the disguise has been dumped; it's around.'

'Where?'

'At a guess, still in the car. We'll go over to the theatre and wait for them to come out after the show.'

Horvarth called in an hour. 'Owes money all over town,' he said. 'Even to Taber. I only had to mention the name to three contacts. They're all keen to get in touch, including, I would think, the mob.'

'They know about it by now.'

THE PARKING LOT behind the theatre had only seven or eight cars so early in the evening. They found the grey subcompact easily. Salter parked his car so as to shield Peterman from the theatre while the sergeant went to work on the trunk. There was a tiny pop and the trunk sprang open. Peterman burrowed through the contents and came up immediately with a bundle wrapped in a dark raincoat. Rolled up inside were a wig, a mouthpiece, some dark glasses, and a mackintosh cap.

'Now we wait,' Salter said. 'Can you close that trunk again?'

WHEN HE EMERGED they had been sitting in Salter's car for five hours. They let him get in his car, then they each opened one of his front doors. Salter spoke to him. 'Can I talk to you Mr Turgeon?'

NINETEEN

TURGEON LOOKED AT HIM, saying nothing.

'Over here. In my car.'

Inside Salter's car, the sergeant held up the bundle. 'This yours?'

'I've never seen it before. What is it?'

'We found it in your trunk.'

'If you found it there you planted it there.'

'That could be, from your lawyer's point of view. So I'll just put all this stuff in a plastic bag and see who the forensic people can connect it to.'

'I recognize Alec's raincoat. I don't know what the other stuff is you planted.'

'Let's go down to my office,' Salter said. 'Give me your keys. Sergeant Peterman will take care of your car. You won't be coming back for a while.'

IT TOOK PETERMAN AN HOUR. When he reappeared in Salter's office he had a pill bottle and a note. Salter took the note and smoothed it out on his desk. It read:

Dear Alec,

Thank you for the pills. You knew what I'd do with them, didn't you? Now I want the whole world to know.

Goodbye,
Mary

THE PRESCRIPTION LABEL on the bottle was made out for Hunter.

'Nice handwriting,' Salter said. 'Where did you find this?'

'Where did *you* find it, you mean? I never saw it before.'

'I was hoping to do this the quick way,' Salter said. 'We've got you on blackmail and murder.'

'I admit I killed him. Self-defence. He deserved it. Now I want to speak to my lawyer.'

'Why did he deserve it? Because he couldn't keep his hands off the women. What are you? Some kind of avenger? Turgeon the Terminator?'

'No, because he killed Mary, and he was going to kill me.'

It was more than Turgeon wanted to say, and it was enough to give Salter the final detail, the one Turgeon didn't know.

'Why do you say that? Because of the pills?' Salter nodded towards the bottle. 'Hunter didn't kill Mary. That bottle had only one pill in it when he gave it to her. She stole the secobarb from Penny Wicklow and tried to get revenge on Hunter by killing herself and writing a note to blame him. You found the note and the bottle and you believed it, so you started to black-mail Hunter, to pay for your own gambling. When he'd had enough, he worked out a way to kill you, a good one. The way he figured it, we'd have found out pretty quickly that you were in debt to the bookies, so we'd have assumed that you were killed by an en-forcer, as we did about Hunter for a while. It must have been quite a shock when Hunter turned on you.

Maybe not, though. You were carrying a knife, weren't you?'

'You forgot to plant that.' Turgeon had recovered from the surprise that Mikhail's note had been her own form of revenge.

Salter said, 'We've got a witness says you followed Hunter at least once to the motel in Brighton. He can identify your car. I don't think you were providing Hunter with alibis. I think you started blackmailing him right then. Letting him know that you'd seen him, asking him for a few dollars to tide you over.'

Turgeon thought this over. 'Actually I did go looking for him once. Connie Spurling had arrived unexpectedly, so I went to look for him to warn him. I knew the motel he used.'

'The witness says you simply circled the motel and drove off.'

'He was looking out the window. I gave him a signal.' Turgeon was getting more and more comfortable. He had seen that it was going to be very hard to get behind his story.

'But when you found the bottle and the note, then you really started milking him. Ten or eleven thousand dollars, Connie Spurling says.'

'That right? He must have been spending a lot on those girls of his. I thought he was gambling.'

Peterman leaned forward. 'The final payoff wasn't money, but the job. You're not qualified for the job, and from what I hear, you aren't much good at it, but Hunter made it a condition of his contract that you would be hired.'

It almost worked. Turgeon said, 'Who told you I wasn't good at the job? I'm *goddam* good at it, I'll tell you,' and then he realized what Peterman was up to and got hold of himself. 'Tell this guy to get lost,' he said to Salter. 'I'll tell you a story.'

The main job was done. They had the man who killed Hunter. What happened in the courtroom would be another story, and Salter understood that Turgeon was offering to satisfy his curiosity, which might otherwise remain forever unsatisfied. He looked at Peterman and nodded, and Peterman looked surprised but left saying nothing.

Turgeon asked for some coffee, which Salter provided. He took his time about beginning, obviously considering what he could say that would be unprovable in court. 'First of all,' he began, 'you have to consider Connie Spurling. She's the real cause. If she hadn't treated me like a piece of shit, I might not have gone along in Hunter's little games, providing his alibis. I *did* provide them, made me feel like a pimp, but anything to upset her I was prepared to do.'

'So you didn't just follow Hunter to the Brighton motel, then start blackmailing him?'

'I'm telling you the truth. I went to warn him that Spurling had arrived early.'

'So you started by covering for Hunter, just as a pal...'

'...because of Spurling...'

'...right. But then you got a little short of cash, and squeezed him.'

'No, get it straight. What he promised to do, what he did, was speak for me in getting the job at the Estragon.'

'So you could continue to cover for him.'

Turgeon looked at Salter thoughtfully. 'You're probably right. I didn't think of that. But I didn't take money for covering for him. I took it because he killed—I thought he killed—Mary Mikhail. There was the note, and the empty bottle. What else could I think?'

'So you thought, "Here's a chance", pocketed the note and the bottle, and started milking him.'

'It took me a few days. A couple of weeks even. I can't tell you now what I had in mind when I pocketed them. I was probably just instinctively covering for him, because it was obviously something he would not want to get out.'

'When did you decide to put the screws to him? Why did you change your mind?'

'I didn't change my mind. I got angry. I liked Mary, and I got angry when I thought he'd killed her, just to get rid of her.'

Salter searched the space between them for the smell of lies. Turgeon was not trying for a righteous air, and he used none of the liar's tricks of noisy protest and emphatic reiteration. Salter was inclined to believe him.

'But you did need money.'

'It was chicken and egg. I wouldn't have asked him if I hadn't needed the money, but it wasn't just because I needed it. I thought he'd killed Mary, so I thought he should pay.'

'Pay you.'

'As you said, I did need the money.'

'How much? How much did you get off him?'

'Altogether?' Turgeon considered. 'About ten thousand.'

So he was probably telling the truth. 'Did you plan to pay him back?'

Now Turgeon smiled. 'No way. It all came from her.'

There was a pause now, as if Turgeon was finished.

'So what happened that night?'

Now there was a longer pause while Turgeon thought through what he was going to say and nodded as if to assure himself. 'I called him on the Saturday, said I had to have a thousand.'

'You're a lousy gambler, you know that?'

'Looks like it, doesn't it? So Alec called back on Sunday saying she'd given him the money and we should meet at this motel, because he'd have the excuse of visiting his aunt to get out of the house. And he said that he thought Spurling was having him followed so we had to meet at a sleazy motel to make it look like he was meeting a bookie. He sounded excited, I could tell he was on a high, and that was what made me think he was giving me a giant crock. And where would she get a thousand on Sunday with all the banks closed? When I'd asked him for the money, I said that Monday would do.

'We'd arranged to meet at eight-thirty. He told me to go to the desk and ask for Mr Rossano. He couldn't use his own name in case somebody recognized the combination of face and name, he said. I said OK. I knew he was up to something. So I drove down early, parked in a quiet spot and waited.

'I nearly missed him. He arrived around eight in Spurling's car. When I saw him get out of the car in that dumb get-up, all I had to do was work it out. It didn't take long. What I couldn't, can't, understand is how he thought he could do it. I'm twice as strong as he is.'

'Maybe he'd been doing push-ups, and I imagine he thought to surprise you. Whose knife was it?'

'Mine. I knew I was walking into something.'

'So you stabbed him, then you garrotted him.'

'No, I stabbed him a couple of times, but he got the knife away from me so I hit him in the face and he went out. I knew I would have to kill him because the whole thing had become a mess, and I wouldn't be able to work here any more. I was pretty sure that you guys would just think it was a whore or pimp in a place like that. Then I realized I could do better than that if I made it look like the guy with the gold tooth had killed him. Use the whole scheme he had planned to kill me. It would have worked. How did you figure out that it was Alec in fancy dress, not some mobster?'

Salter ignored the question. 'So then you took off his make-up and garrotted him?'

'He already took it all off, waiting for me. It was all wrapped up in the bundle you found in my car. That tooth thing and his clothes, his raincoat. And the glasses and moustache and stuff. He had a make-up kit in his car which had the cleaning cream I needed.'

'You garrotted him first?'

Turgeon shook his head. 'No, first I cleaned off the bit of make-up. I didn't want to get it on the sash-cord. He was unconscious.'

'You were really thinking straight, weren't you?'

Turgeon began to smile but there was no admiration in Salter's voice, and he checked himself. 'The guy planned to kill me,' Turgeon said, and now the righteous tone appeared.

And that was that. Salter said, 'I'll have you dictate a statement.'

'You'll do what?' Turgeon didn't even shout. 'Why do you think I told your pal to make himself scarce? I haven't told you a thing. Now I want a lawyer. You can bring your pal back, too.'

TURGEON ALMOST GOT AWAY with it. On the witness stand he denied any suggestion that he had ever taken money from Hunter, insisting, rather, that Hunter was in his debt. He went to the motel, he said, to take some money to Hunter to pay off a bookie. He had lent him money before. In fact, he said, Hunter owed him quite a lot. When he arrived, he was attacked by Hunter and forced to defend himself. Hunter had a knife which Turgeon got away from him, and then Hunter attacked him with the cord. After he realized Hunter was dead he panicked, of course, before he saw that if he took away the make-up and costume it would be assumed that Hunter was killed by the Mafia, a fate Hunter had intended for Turgeon. He did this because, although he felt innocent, he knew that a jury might decide against him. He thought that the reason Hunter would want to kill him was to get rid of his debt to Turgeon which was in the thousands. He knew Hunter was capable of it because of what he'd done to Mary Mikhail.

Tell us, the defence lawyer demanded, about the death of Mary Mikhail.

Turgeon did so, ending up agreeing that he had pocketed the bottle and the note as the act of a friend, to preserve Hunter's reputation in the theatrical community and to avoid damaging his relationship with Miss Spurling. He had then promptly forgotten about them.

'Did you tell Hunter you had them?'

'Of course, I told him that I'd found them in the room.'

'And you still had them?'

'No. He asked me for them and I looked around but I couldn't find them, so I promised him I'd destroy them if they turned up.'

The prosecution then put it to him that he had not lost the pill and the note, but had kept them to blackmail Hunter, extorting so much money that Hunter was driven to try to get rid of him.

'No, sir,' Turgeon said. 'I *did* ask him to repay a little of the money I'd lent him, and that's when he decided to wipe out the whole debt.'

At one point the defence lawyer asked him to describe his attitude to Hunter, and Turgeon said he was extremely grateful to Hunter for his present job, and continued to depend on him to put in a good word when the company moved to Chicago. When Hunter left the company, he felt very unprotected in view of his limited experience and the great competition for jobs in the theatre.

It was impossible to disprove that Hunter was pursued by bookmakers, just as it was impossible to disprove Turgeon's assertion that he himself never gambled. Horvarth had been unable to find a bookmaker willing to stand up and identify himself in court. Only the fact that the jury found it hard to swallow that Turgeon, having stabbed Hunter, still found it necessary to garrotte him in self-defence secured the conviction. His lawyer pointed out that there could be no question of premeditation, and anyway Turgeon believed he needed Hunter to speak for him when the play moved to Chicago. Ironically, Perry Adler spoke for him as a character witness: he said that Turgeon was a very fine stage manager and owed no part of his job to Hunter's influence. Turgeon was sentenced to two years for manslaughter.

AFTER THE TRIAL, Salter joined Peterman and Marinelli for coffee to talk over the case.

'It was just a hunch, wasn't it?' Peterman asked.

'It was a lot of little hunches. First of all he stuck too long to the story that Hunter was a gambler, and he was close enough to Hunter to know he wasn't. Then he said that Brighton was too small a town to have a bookie. How would he know that? The thing that stuck with me when I was wondering about the drugs was that he was the only one who said he *didn't* go into Mikhail's room. Can you believe that anyone seeing Mikhail sprawled out on a bed, maybe dead, maybe not, would stay in the doorway?' Salter consulted a piece of paper. 'That was about it. The list kept growing. Of course, for a long time the trouble was he was the wrong shape. Dick here cleared that up.'

Peterman looked at Salter, astonished. 'When?'

'When you suggested that maybe it was Hunter who had persuaded the killer to come and meet him.'

'It was just a thought,' Peterman said modestly. Then he grinned. 'I don't even remember saying it.'

'But how did you connect the girl's death with the case in the first place?' Marinelli asked. 'Another hunch?'

'Sort of. When I realized that Hunter didn't get into heavy debt until after Mikhail died.'

Marinelli sat back and looked at the two other policemen. 'If you hadn't found the stuff in his car, you'd have been up shit creek.'

'We knew he'd done it. We'd have got there eventually. Sergeant Peterman would have talked to him for a few days. Right, Dick?'

'That's sometimes what it takes.'

To THE DEPUTY CHIEF, Salter made a point of stressing Horvarth's contribution, and detected in Mackenzie a small softening of attitude which he interpreted and translated back to Horvarth as a probable indicator that Horvarth would be back on the gambling squad after a reasonable penance in Community Relations.

RANOVIC CALLED. When they had got Hunter's story out of the way, Salter asked, 'Sorted out your own life yet?'

'In a way,' Ranovic said. 'She had a miscarriage two days ago. That's really why I called.'

'Jesus, I'm sorry.'

'Yeah, she's OK, though. I thought it was the end of the world. I wanted to take her down to the Caribbean for a couple of weeks to recover, but she just took it in her stride. It happens to a lot of women, she said. She sounded like my grandmother. But it's got a bright side. We're going to get married. See, now there's no reason for me to marry her, except that I want to, she's satisfied it's the right thing to do. And we're going to have a baby as soon as possible.'

'She's going to stay home?'

'We haven't decided yet. We'll both apply for maternal leave.'

'Do we have that in the force?'

'If we don't, we will. This new government is very big on stuff like that. Will you come?'

'Sure. Just tell me what to expect.'

THREE WEEKS LATER Annie returned. Her father's condition was stable. They could expect some mild improvement with therapy, but he would probably never be able to look after himself again, and Annie had got him settled into a nursing home. Angus, she reported, was staying on the Island with her mother.

'What about the girl?'

'She's staying with Mother, too.'

'Your mother going to be the chaperone?'

'They are sharing a bedroom.'

'In the family mansion?'

'Angus laid it out to Mother as soon as he decided to stay. The boys are tickled pink to have a male in the next generation interested in the business. They've adopted him, and there I think he'll stay. Mother, too, is delighted. Never mind the morality.'

'You mean he just told her he was sleeping with Linda, and your mother said, "Good boy, don't fight"?'

'More or less.'

'Christ. She's ruthless, you know that. She'll do anything to get us down there. She knows she's wasting her time with me, so she took Angus at any price, including a live-in girlfriend. So much for the old maritime values.'

'There are other ways of putting it.'

'I know. I'm sorry. I visited an old folks' home. I know how she feels. But she'd still like to see the rest of us down there?'

'Yes.'

'See?'

'How's Seth?'

'Happy as a clam. Here. In Toronto.'

'How's the job been?'

He told her about the case, ending by telling her he wanted to watch television the following Saturday afternoon. The local cable company was televising the finals of Peterman's tango competition.

'How about you?' she asked. 'Been dancing yourself?'

An odd question that should have warned him. 'No. Why? Dancing?'

'I just wondered if the lady you took to Niagara Falls also dances.'

'Who told you about her?'

'Mary Sacher. She called me to see if I knew of a place she could rent for the summer on the Island. And told me all the gossip. Somebody saw you at Niagara Falls with a woman no one knows.'

'Ah. Yeah. Well. Let me tell you who that was...'

SET-UP
Maxine
O'Callaghan

CROSSFIRE

It began with a set-up. Los Angeles private investigator Delilah West goes undercover in the county supervisor's office to smoke out the employee siphoning funds. Guilty party nailed. Case closed.

That is, until the woman Delilah fingered is murdered, and Delilah's new client—an Orange County councilwoman— is the prime suspect. Worse, Delilah lied to protect her client. The only way to save both their skins is to flush out the real killer.

"Nothing daunts Delilah West...." —*Los Angeles Times*

Available in May at your favorite retail stores.

To order your copy, please send your name, address, zip or postal code, along with a check or money order for $3.99 (please do not send cash), plus 75¢ postage and handling ($1.00 in Canada) for each book ordered, payable to Worldwide Mystery, to:

In the U.S.

Worldwide Mystery
3010 Walden Ave.
P. O. Box 1325
Buffalo, NY 14269-1325

In Canada

Worldwide Mystery
P. O. Box 609
Fort Erie, Ontario
L2A 5X3

Please specify book title with your order.
Canadian residents add applicable federal and provincial taxes.

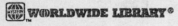 **WORLDWIDE LIBRARY**®

SET-UP

DANCING IN THE DARK
Sharon Zukowski
A Blaine Stewart Mystery

(First Time in Paperback)

HIGH STEAKS

After a steady diet of coffee, cigarettes and too much paperwork, New York private investigator Blaine Stewart was hungry for undercover work. The place was WARM—Worldwide Animal Rights Movement—and they had a bone to pick with cattle rancher Jacob Faradeux.

The corporate carnivore hires Blaine to stop any nasty surprises these activists have planned for his stock-exchange debut.

But now a mad bomber is leaving deadly packages that are ripping apart Blaine's life. Is WARM behind it—or someone else with a more personal score to settle? The answer lies in a scorching revelation about Blaine's past...and meat isn't the only thing that's going to burn.

"Flinty and well paced." *—Booklist*

Available in July at your favorite retail stores.

To order your copy, please send your name, address, zip or postal code, along with a check or money order for $3.99 (please do not send cash), plus 75¢ postage and handling ($1.00 in Canada) for each book ordered, payable to Worldwide Mystery, to:

In the U.S.	In Canada
Worldwide Mystery	Worldwide Mystery
3010 Walden Ave.	P. O. Box 609
P. O. Box 1325	Fort Erie, Ontario
Buffalo, NY 14269-1325	L2A 5X3

Please specify book title with your order.
Canadian residents add applicable federal and provincial taxes.

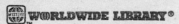 WORLDWIDE LIBRARY®

DANCING

A JOHN COFFIN MYSTERY

First Time in Paperback

Gwendoline Butler

DANGEROUS TWISTS AND TURNS

The crimes begin in a bizarre fashion. First, a busload of tipsy sightseers braving London's terror tour disappears on notorious "Murder Street." Next, a child's stuffed toy is kidnapped, brutalized and buried.

For Scotland Yard Inspector John Coffin, things go from odd to alarming when the tour bus is found, its passengers alive except for one—an armchair crime enthusiast who has been murdered. Worse, the young son of a visiting American actress disappears in the wake of a series of child abductions.

But nothing is as it seems—not the people, not the events on Murder Street, which Coffin fears may continue to live up to its bloody history.

"Butler...keeps the reader moving quickly...."
—*Publishers Weekly*

Available in July at your favorite retail stores.

To order your copy, please send your name, address, zip or postal code, along with a check or money order for $3.99 (please do not send cash), plus 75¢ postage and handling ($1.00 in Canada) for each book ordered, payable to Worldwide Mystery, to:

In the U.S.	In Canada
Worldwide Mystery	Worldwide Mystery
3010 Walden Ave.	P. O. Box 609
P. O. Box 1325	Fort Erie, Ontario
Buffalo, NY 14269-1325	L2A 5X3

Please specify book title with your order.
Canadian residents add applicable federal and provincial taxes

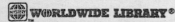 **WORLDWIDE LIBRARY**®

MURDER

WILLFUL INTENT

Gambling had been Muriel's life—it had destroyed her marriage and very nearly her husband's career. Now, in death, Muriel has taken her biggest gamble of all. A deathbed revision of her will leaves everything, including several Las Vegas casinos and a cache of valuable rubies, to ex-husband Lennox Kemp. In doing so, she stiffed some *very* powerful men.

But both the jewels and the second will are missing. So is the nurse who cared for Muriel. Now, with murder and the Mob on his doorstep, English solicitor Lennox Kemp gets a taste of the action—Nevada-style.

"Meek never fails to be engaging...."
—*Cleveland Plain Dealer*

Available in June at your favorite retail stores.

TOUCH & GO

M.R.D. MEEK

A Lennox Kemp Mystery

First Time in Paperback

To order your copy, please send your name, address, zip or postal code, along with a check or money order for $3.99 (please do not send cash), plus 75¢ postage and handling ($1.00 in Canada) for each book ordered, payable to Worldwide Mystery, to:

In the U.S.	In Canada
Worldwide Mystery	Worldwide Mystery
3010 Walden Ave.	P. O. Box 609
P. O. Box 1325	Fort Erie, Ontario
Buffalo, NY 14269-1325	L2A 5X3

Please specify book title with your order.
Canadian residents add applicable federal and provincial taxes.

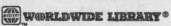 **WORLDWIDE LIBRARY®**